Bofuri

LILY

Lily's STATS

Lv86
HP 340/340
MP 170/170
[STR 100]
[VIT 30]
[AGI 60]
[DEX 30]
[INT 100]

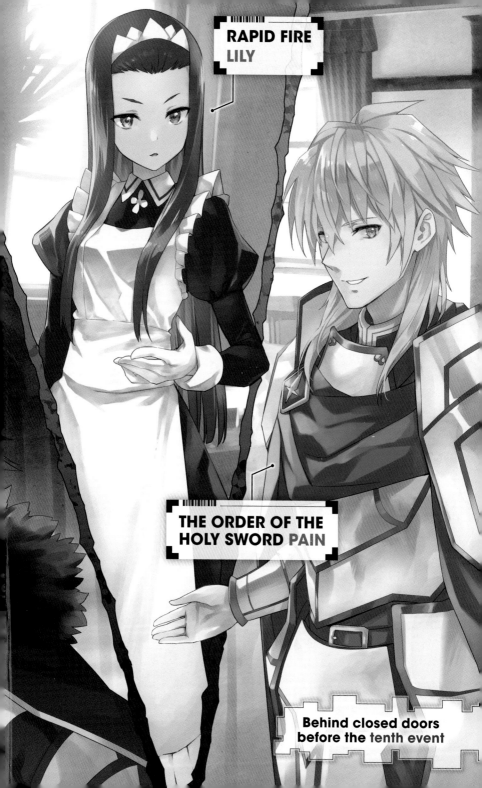

RAPID FIRE
LILY

THE ORDER OF THE
HOLY SWORD PAIN

Behind closed doors
before the tenth event

"Is that enough? Okay, Ancient Weapon!"

The cubes released tiny blue flames, like sparks—but an instant later, they extended into strands of blue light, like the bars of a cage.

In a dark forest

Skills

Quick Change / Sharpness / Armor Spear / Shake Off
Spear Mastery VII / Magic Mastery VII
Servant Boost (L) / HP Boost (L) / MP Boost (L)
Attack Boost (M) / Magic Boost / Fast Chant / Fire Magic V
Water Magic V / Wind Magic V / Earth Magic V / Dark Magic V
Light Magic V / Poison Nullification / Paralyze Nullification
Stun Nullification / Sleep Resist (L) / Freeze Resist (L)
Burn Resist (L) / Throw / Mind's Eye / Leap / Diving VI
Swimming VI / Venerable Command / Tactical Tutelage
Gate Buster / Strong Legion / Reproduction / Occupation

Bofuri

★ I Don't ★
Want to Get
Hurt, so I'll
⑬ Max Out My
Defense.

YUUMIKAN

Illustration by KOIN

YEN ON
NEW YORK

LILY'S STATS

Lily
Lv 86   HP 340/340   MP 170/170
[STR 100]   [VIT 30]   [AGI 60]
[DEX 30]   [INT 100]

Welcome to
NewWorld Online.

Bofuri I Don't Want to Get Hurt, so I'll Max Out My Defense.

YUUMIKAN

Translation by Andrew Cunningham • Cover art by Koin

ITAINO WA IYA NANODE BOGYORYOKU NI KYOKUFURI SHITAITO OMOIMASU. Vol. 13
©Yuumikan, Koin 2022
First published in Japan in 2022 by KADOKAWA CORPORATION, Tokyo.
English translation rights arranged with KADOKAWA CORPORATION, Tokyo, through TUTTLE-MORI AGENCY, INC., Tokyo.

English translation © 2024 by Yen Press, LLC

Yen On
150 West 30th Street, 19th Floor
New York, NY 10001

Visit us at yenpress.com • facebook.com/yenpress • twitter.com/yenpress
yenpress.tumblr.com • instagram.com/yenpress

First Yen On Edition: July 2024
Edited by Yen On Editorial: Leilah Labossiere, Ivan Liang
Designed by Yen Press Design: Liz Parlett

Yen On is an imprint of Yen Press, LLC.
The Yen On name and logo are trademarks of Yen Press, LLC.

Library of Congress Cataloging-in-Publication Data
Names: Yuumikan, author. I Koin, illustrator. I Cunningham, Andrew, 1979– translator.
Title: Bofuri, I don't want to get hurt, so I'll max out my defense / Yuumikan ; illustration by Koin ; translated by Andrew Cunningham.
Other titles: Itai no wa iya nano de bōgyoryoku ni kyokufuri shitai to omoimasu. English
Description: First Yen On edition. I New York : Yen On, 2021–
Identifiers: LCCN 2020055872 I ISBN 9781975322731 (v. 1 ; trade paperback) I
    ISBN 9781975323547 (v. 2 ; trade paperback) I ISBN 9781975323561 (v. 3 ; trade paperback) I
    ISBN 9781975323585 (v. 4 ; trade paperback) I ISBN 9781975323608 (v. 5 ; trade paperback) I
    ISBN 9781975323622 (v. 6 ; trade paperback) I ISBN 9781975323646 (v. 7 ; trade paperback) I
    ISBN 9781975323660 (v. 8 ; trade paperback) I ISBN 9781975323684 (v. 9 ; trade paperback) I
    ISBN 9781975367688 (v. 10 ; trade paperback) I ISBN 9781975367701 (v. 11 ; trade paperback) I
    ISBN 9781975367725 (v. 12 ; trade paperback) I ISBN 9781975367749 (v. 13 ; trade paperback)
Subjects: LCSH: Video gamers—Fiction. I Virtual reality—Fiction. I GSAFD: Science fiction.
Classification: LCC PL874.I46 I8313 2021 I DDC 895.63/6—dc23
LC record available at https://lccn.loc.gov/2020055872

ISBNs: 978-1-9753-6774-9 (paperback)
       978-1-9753-6775-6 (ebook)

10 9 8 7 6 5 4 3 2 1

LSC-C

Printed in the United States of America

CONTENTS

**I Don't Want to Get Hurt,
so I'll Max Out My Defense.**

NewWorld Online Status ‖ GUILD **Maple Tree**

‖ NAME **Maple** LV **70**

HP **200/200**   MP **22/22**

PROFILE
The Tankiest Great Shielder

She was a gaming noob, but by putting all her points in defense, she grew so tanky that all attacks just bounce right off. The kind of girl who finds fun in everything, her imaginative leaps astound those around her. When she fights, she negates all incoming attacks while unleashing a barrage of counter-skills.

STATUS

[STR] **000** [VIT] **19560** [AGI] **000**

[DEX] **000** [INT] **000**

EQUIPMENT

‖ New Moon: Hydra   ‖ Bonding Bridge

‖ Night's Facsimile: Devour/Lure of the Deep

‖ Black Rose Armor: Saturating Chaos

‖ Toughness Ring   ‖ Life Ring

SKILLS

Shield Attack   Sidestep   Deflect   Meditation   Taunt   Inspire   HP Boost (S)   MP Boost (S)   Heavy Body

Green's Grace   Great Shield Mastery X   Cover Move V   Cover   Pierce Guard   Counter   Quick Change

Absolute Defense   Moral Turpitude   Sheep Eater   Hydra Eater   Bomb Eater   Indomitable Guardian

Giant Killing   Psychokinesis   Fortress   Martyr's Devotion   Machine God   Bug Urn Curse   Zone Freeze

Pandemonium I   Heaven's Throne   Nether Nexus   Crystallization   Cataclysmic Eruption   Unbreakable Shield

Twisted Resurrection   Earth Wielding II   Apex of Authority   Glow of Deliverance

TAMED MONSTER

‖ Name **Syrup**   A turtle with high defense

Giganticize   Spirit Cannon   Mother Nature   etc.

NewWorld Online Status ‖ GUILD **Maple Tree**

‖ NAME **Sally** ‖ LV **74**

HP 32/32 MP 130/130

PROFILE
The Unhittable Assassin

Maple's friend and partner, she's got a good head on her shoulders. Her top priority is to ensure she and Maple enjoy the game together. Light armor and twin daggers are the core of her combat style; her raw gaming talent and astonishing focus allow her to evade all attacks.

STATUS

STR 150 VIT 000 AGI 185
DEX 045 INT 060

EQUIPMENT

‖ Deep Sea Dagger   ‖ Seabed Dagger

‖ Surface Scarf: Mirage   ‖ Oceanic Coat: Oceanic

‖ Oceanic Clothes   ‖ Bonding Bridge

‖ Charnel Boots: One Step in the Grave

SKILLS

Gale Slash	Defense Break	Inspire	Down Attack	Power Attack	Switch Attack	Pinpoint Attack
Combo Blade V	Martial Arts VIII	Fire Magic III	Water Magic III	Wind Magic III	Earth Magic III	
Dark Magic III	Light Magic III	Strength Boost (L)	Combo Boost (L)	MP Boost (L)	MP Cost Down (L)	
MP Recovery Speed Boost (L)	Poison Resist (S)	Gathering Speed Boost (S)	Dagger Mastery X			
Magic Mastery III	Dagger Secrets V	Affliction VIII	Presence Block III	Presence Detect II		
Sneaky Steps I	Leap V	Quick Change	Cooking I	Fishing	Swimming X	Diving X	Shearing
Superspeed	Ancient Ocean	Chaser Blade	Jack of All Trades	Sword Dance	Shed Skin	
Web Spinner IX	Ice Pillar	Subzero Domain	Nether Nexus	Cataclysmic Eruption	Water Wielding VII	
Substitute						

TAMED MONSTER

‖ Name **Oboro**   A fox with skills that bewilder foes

Fleeting Shadow   Shadow Clone   Binding Barrier   etc.

NewWorld Online Status ‖ GUILD **Maple Tree**

‖ NAME **Chrome** LV **90**

HP 940/940 MP 52/52

PROFILE
The Unstoppable, Unyielding Zombie Tank

Known as a top player since the early days of *NewWorld Online*. Reliable, caring, everyone's big brother. Like Maple, he's a Great Shielder. His unique gear gives him a 50 percent chance of surviving any hit with 1 HP, and he has a ton of healing skills that make him extremely tenacious.

STATUS

STR **140** VIT **200** AGI **040**

DEX **030** INT **020**

EQUIPMENT

‖ Headhunter: Life Eater

‖ Wrath Wraith Wall: Soul Syphon

‖ Bloodstained Skull: Soul Eater

‖ Bloodstained Bone Armor: Dead or Alive

‖ Robust Ring   ‖ Impregnable Ring

‖ Bonding Bridge

SKILLS

Thrust Elemental Blade Shield Attack Sidestep Deflect Great Defense Taunt Bulwark

Impregnable Stance Iron Body Guardian Heavy Body HP Boost (L) HP Recovery Speed Boost (L) Cover

MP Boost (L) Green's Grace Great Shield Mastery X Defense Mastery X Cover Move X Multi-Cover

Pierce Guard Counter Guard Aura Defensive Formation Guardian Power Great Shield Secrets X

Defense Secrets IX Burn Resist (L) Stun Nullification Paralyze Nullification Poison Nullification

Sleep Nullification Freeze Nullification Mining IV Gathering VII Shearing Swimming V Diving V

Spirit Light Indomitable Guardian Battle Healing Reaper's Mire Crystallization Stimulation

TAMED MONSTER

‖ Name **Necro** An armor monster that really shines when worn

Polterguard Impact Reflection etc.

I Don't Want to Get Hurt, so I'll Max Out My Defense

Welcome to *NewWorld Online*

NewWorld Online Status | ‖ GUILD **Maple Tree**

‖ NAME **Iz** | LV **73**

HP 100/100 MP 100/100

PROFILE
The Ultimate Crafter

A specialized crafter, she's proud of her work and particular about the results. Her gaming style is all about making clothes, weapons, armor, and items. Originally, she wasn't that active in combat, but her stock of attack and support items now makes a huge difference.

STATUS

STR 045 VIT 020 AGI 095

DEX 210 INT 085

EQUIPMENT

‖ Blacksmith Hammer X

‖ Alchemist Goggles: Faustian Alchemy

‖ Alchemist Long Coat: Magic Workshop

‖ Blacksmith Leggings X

‖ Alchemist Boots: New Frontier ‖ Potion Pouch

‖ Item Pouch ‖ Bonding Bridge

SKILLS

Strike Crafting Mastery X Crafting Secrets X Enhance Success Rate Boost (L) Gathering Speed Boost (L)

Mining Speed Boost (L) Crafting Quantity Boost (L) Crafting Speed Boost (L) Affliction III Sneaky Steps V

Keen Sight Smithing X Sewing X Horticulture X Synthesizing X Augmentation X Cooking X

Mining X Gathering X Swimming X Diving X Shearing Godsmith's Grace X Observer's Eye

Attribute Endowment VII Botany Mineralogy

TAMED MONSTER

‖ Name **Fey** A spirit that helps with item creation

Item Boost Recycle etc.

On't Want to Get Hurt, so I'll Max Out My Defense.

elcome to NewWorld Online

NewWorld Online Status ‖ GUILD **Maple Tree**

‖ NAME **Kasumi** LV **86**

HP 435/435 MP 70/70

PROFILE
The Solitary Sword Dancer

A katana-wielding female player with a strong knack for solo play. Always calm, she's good at assessing the big picture. Yet she's frequently left reeling by Maple's and Sally's outlandish antics. Has a range of katana skills that let her contribute to almost any combat situation.

STATUS

‖STR‖ 205 ‖VIT‖ 080 ‖AGI‖ 120

‖DEX‖ 030 ‖INT‖ 030

EQUIPMENT

‖ Yukari, the All-Consuming Blight

‖ Cherry Blossom Barrette

‖ Cherry Blossom Vestments

‖ Edo Purple Hakama ‖ Samurai Greaves

‖ Samurai Gauntlets ‖ Gold Obi Fastener

‖ Cherry Blossom Crest ‖ Bonding Bridge

SKILLS

Gleam · Helmsplitter · Guard Break · Sweep Slice · Eye for Attack · Inspire · Attack Stance · Katana Arts X · Cleave · Throw · Power Aura · Armor Slicer · HP Boost (L) · MP Boost (M) · Attack Boost (L) · Poison Nullification · Paralyze Nullification · Stun Resist (L) · Sleep Resist (L) · Freeze Resist (M) · Burn Resist (L) · Longsword Mastery X · Katana Mastery X · Longsword Secrets VIII · Katana Secrets VIII · Mining IV · Gathering VI · Diving VIII · Swimming VIII · Leap VII · Shearing · Keen Sight · Indomitable · Sword Spirit · Dauntless · Sinew · Superspeed · Ever Vigilant · Mind's Eye · Specter of Carnage

TAMED MONSTER

‖ Name **Haku**   A white snake that ambushes foes from the mist

Supergiant · Paralytoxin · etc.

NewWorld Online Status

‖ GUILD **Maple Tree**

‖ NAME **Kanade** LV **62**

HP 335/335 **MP** 250/250

PROFILE
The Whimsical Genius Mage

A certifiable genius with an androgynous look and a memory beyond compare. His mind once left him avoiding human contact, but Maple's innocent cheer broke through that shell. He can store all manner of spells in the grimoires on his book stacks, ready for use in combat.

STATUS

STR 015 **VIT** 010 **AGI** 095
DEX 050 **INT** 135

EQUIPMENT

‖ Divine Wisdom: Akashic Records

‖ Diamond Newsboy Cap VIII

‖ Smart Coat VI   ‖ Smart Leggings VIII

‖ Smart Boots VI   ‖ Spade Earrings

‖ Mage Gloves   ‖ Bonding Bridge

SKILLS

Magic Mastery VIII   Fast Chant   MP Boost (L)   MP Cost Down (L)   MP Recovery Speed Boost (L)

Magic Boost (L)   Green's Grace   Fire Magic VII   Water Magic V   Wind Magic IX   Earth Magic V

Dark Magic III   Light Magic VIII   Swimming V   Diving V   Sorcerer's Stacks   Technical Archive

Reaper's Mire   Magic Meld

TAMED MONSTER

‖ Name **Sou**   A slime that can copy a player's abilities

Mimic   Divide   etc.

NewWorld Online Status

‖ NAME **Mai**

LV **56**

HP 35/35   MP 20/20

PROFILE
Conquerer Twin

A beginner player with an extreme attack build, she and her younger twin sister, Yui, were scouted by Maple. She does her best to help everyone out. The twins have the highest DPS in the game, and their dual-wielding hammers vaporize anything that gets close.

STATUS

[STR] 515   [VIT] 000   [AGI] 000

[DEX] 000   [INT] 000

EQUIPMENT

‖ Black Annihilammer X   ‖ Black Doll Dress X

‖ Black Doll Tights X   ‖ Black Doll Shoes X

‖ Little Ribbon   ‖ Silk Gloves

‖ Bonding Bridge

SKILLS

Double Stamp   Double Impact   Double Strike   Attack Boost (L)   Hammer Mastery X   Hammer Secrets I

Throw   Farshot   Conqueror   Annihilator   Giant Killing   Destroy Mode   Titan's Lot

TAMED MONSTER

‖ Name. **Tsukimi**   A bear monster with distinctive black fur

Power Share   Bright Star   etc.

I Don't Want to Get Hurt, so I'll Max Out My Defense

Welcome to NewWorld Online

NewWorld Online Status ‖ GUILD **Maple Tree**

‖ NAME **Yui** LV **56**

HP 35/35   MP 20/20

PROFILE
Annihilator Twin

A beginner player with an extreme attack build, she and her older twin sister, Mai, were scouted by Maple. She's more positive than Mai and quicker to recover. The twins have the highest DPS in the game. Throwing Iz's custom-made iron balls lets them take out enemies at range.

STATUS

STR 515   VIT 000   AGI 000
DEX 000   INT 000

EQUIPMENT

‖ White Annihilammer X   ‖ White Doll Dress X
‖ White Doll Tights X   ‖ White Doll Shoes X
‖ Little Ribbon   ‖ Silk Gloves
‖ Bonding Bridge

SKILLS

Double Stamp   Double Impact   Double Strike   Attack Boost (L)   Hammer Mastery X   Hammer Secrets I
Throw   Farshot   Conqueror   Annihilator   Giant Killing   Destroy Mode   Titan's Lot

TAMED MONSTER

‖ Name **Yukimi**   A bear monster with distinctive white fur

Power Share   Bright Star   etc.

Prologue

The eighth stratum had been almost entirely underwater. Every dungeon started with a dive, getting around required boats, and Diving and Swimming skills were a must for effective exploration—not exactly a location Maple was built for. Still, there were plenty of players as unskilled as her, and the designers had provided a solution. Maple bought a diving suit that could only be used on the eighth stratum, which granted her a degree of underwater mobility.

As the players upgraded the suits, their effective range expanded, and they soon began finding dungeons deep below the waves. Sally tackled one such dungeon solo and fought a boss that was all about water currents and bolts of light, but she dodged them all and obtained a second unique set of gear.

Sally's new equipment provided exactly the kind of new skills she'd been hoping for. They were focused on illusions, perfect for playing tricks on human opponents. They weren't easy to use, but if done right, she could pry open a foe's defenses. For the girl who'd once convinced Frederica she had a skill that wasn't even real—well, this was exactly Sally's style.

There were even more treasures hidden on that ocean floor:

Kanade found an upgrade for his wand, and Maple found an ancient weapon that added to her offensive skill set.

They refined their teamwork while getting used to their new skills. Playing off one another's strengths, the eight members of Maple Tree easily cleared the boss in the dungeon leading to the ninth stratum and set foot on the new map. The ninth stratum was divided into twin lands, one side filled with water and nature, and the other a barren land of fire.

Ever since the fourth stratum was implemented, the player base had been growing steadily more powerful. With that in mind, the next event was going to be a large-scale PvP battle. Velvet had already announced she was going to pick the opposite side—Thunder Storm was out to fight Maple Tree. Top guilds (like Maple Tree) were the subject of widespread scrutiny.

Whatever plans each guild had, this stratum would be their final chance to prepare for the oncoming war.

CHAPTER 1

Defense Build and the Twin Lands

At the entrance to the ninth stratum, Maple Tree was faced with a choice. Every previous map had a single town, but this one had *two*.

On one side was a wasteland of bare rocks and jagged mountain peaks. Plumes of flame rose from the ground, and lightning flashed overhead—truly a rugged landscape. In the distance, they could see a town surrounding a splendid castle; it was pitch-black but decorated with motifs representing the fire and lightning all around.

In the opposite direction was an expanse of green, columns of water, and chunks of floating ice—the bounty of nature. The town was all white, and even decorated with water and more ice, giving it a very tranquil look.

"Which way do we go?"

"I doubt they're much different functionally, but vibes are important. We should go with whichever you like best."

"Right now, we don't really know anything. I doubt we'll be locked in the moment we set foot inside, so we could just try them both out."

The admins had not issued any warnings about this choice.

Which meant it was unlikely they'd be forced to pick a base of operations right off the bat.

"Then…let's start with the forest!"

Maple pointed toward the wooded area where water flowed freely between the trees. Bridges and staircases made of ice dotted the landscape.

"Okay, gotta start somewhere."

"I bet each area has different materials."

"Yeah, we'll have to explore both to get everything."

With two different zones, each quite large, there was no shortage of places to visit.

"Let's get going!"

"Yui, don't run ahead!"

"Come on, Maple."

"Yeah! I guess we take these stairs?"

They headed down into the woods below.

Creeks crisscrossed the forest floor, while babbling brooks and small ponds could be found all over the zone. The sounds of water were everywhere. There were even pools of water floating in the air, like Sally's Waterway. There'd been similar-looking monsters on previous maps, but these were different.

"Not monsters! Just a terrain feature."

"There are ice lumps floating over there. And pillars!"

They'd seen those from above, but they didn't seem related to any monster locations.

Perhaps they were just there to mirror the lava on the other half of the map.

"We're almost at the town—let's not get sidetracked until we hit our Guild Home. Given the choice of towns, I'm assuming we'll have a home in each."

"True. Let's go there first!"

They didn't see any monsters on the way, so they quickly reached their destination.

"I thought as much from up above, but this place sure is different from the previous stratums."

"Such huge walls! Sally, do you think they go all the way around?"

"Most likely. That's sort of what walls do."

The town was surrounded by towering fortifications, which were in turn ringed by a moat. The group was close enough now to see the drawbridge leading into the town proper.

It was a much clearer boundary between town and field than on any previous map.

As they crossed the drawbridge, they noticed a crystal above the gate, radiating a pale light. It didn't seem to be doing much of anything yet, so they kept on moving.

The entrance itself was flanked with NPCs in full plate armor— town guards.

"Travelers? Once you've found lodgings, visit the castle in the center of town."

"Will do!" Maple shouted excitedly, and she was the first to set foot inside.

Several previous areas had featured towns heavily influenced by the stratum theme. This one on the ninth floor was more of a standard European castle town—beautiful and filled with those strange floating water and ice sculptures, but otherwise mostly normal.

After the underwater village on the eighth stratum, it felt like a while since they'd been anywhere this ordinary.

"Oh, it actually gave us a quest," Chrome said. "That's a new one."

Everyone checked, and they did have *Head to the castle* in their logs.

"This floor might be designed around following a questline. If they're giving it to us automatically, probably unwise to ignore it."

"Yeah, definitely demands attention."

"Then after we hit up the Guild Home, shall we visit the castle together?"

"Good idea!"

"Let's do that, Maple!"

Mai and Yui ran off after Maple. The other five followed close behind. Those three who took off first were so slow that even if they ran, the rest of the guild could easily keep up.

"I assume everyone's gonna get the main quest. Wonder how heavily it branches off into the sub-quests?"

"I'll check out the other town as soon as I get a chance," Kanade offered. "It'll be easier to plan if we know the full scope."

"I think I'll join you," Iz said. "If Maple's planning on exploring this side, I'm sure she and anyone with her will get enough materials; plus I'd like to get the full range as soon as I can."

"Kasumi and I'll help explore," Chrome said. "We're the old reliables; but if luck's a factor, best to leave it those three."

"I like how that's our default assumption now."

"If they just go out and have fun like always, it'll all end well."

"Yup."

As Maple and the twins led the way, the rest of them discussed PvP prep. The trio's extreme builds were powerful—but they couldn't let them do all the work. Good results required careful preparation.

Sally had never been one to shy away from planning and was ready to do everything in her power to make sure they had a proper strategy.

*   *   *

After a stop at their Guild Home, they followed the quest prompt and headed to the castle.

"Sally, Sally, is that it?"

"Has to be, right?"

They were walking along the road to the distant castle, which was as beautiful as it was towering.

The road leading to it was quite broad, filled not only with other players but also with throngs of NPCs. Quite the bustling thoroughfare.

"The town itself is unusually large. And I thought the fourth stratum's was big."

That map had featured a town of everlasting night and had strict conditions that determined progress toward the center. Once all areas were unlocked, it was the largest town the game offered, but this one was clearly comparable.

"I think this place might be even bigger. It's gonna take a while to see what it has to offer."

As they followed the road to the castle, the view of the town opened around them. The streets ran right up against the town walls, and this was hardly the only broad avenue. There were likely all sorts of little shops to find in every direction.

"And since the other side has its own town, that's double the locations."

Sally was right—the fire and lightning side had a town, too. If the two halves of the map were meant to mirror each other, it was probably just as big.

"Wow…guess we'll have to work together to scope things out!"

The areas outside of towns were vast, but no previous floors had featured such spacious towns.

Obviously, they couldn't neglect the fields—but previous floors had shown the towns were full of hints and quests.

"I'm your town research guy," Kanade said.

"Again."

"Ah-ha-ha, yeah."

"With a town this size, we'll never get bored, even if we're not out fighting."

As they spoke, they continued climbing; at last, they reached the foot of the castle proper. The path led through the open gates, gardens sprawling on either side.

Like the town entrance, the gates were flanked by guard NPCs, who spoke up as Maple Tree approached.

"Travelers? You've chosen a curious time to visit."

"I wonder what that means, Sally!"

"Good question. Could be related to the event."

"I'll be your guide. Follow me."

One of the guards led them inside. With no reason to linger, they all filed along after.

The castle interior was quite elaborate, and they were led down corridor after corridor, every wall, floor, and ceiling lavishly decorated.

"Are we allowed in the other halls?"

"Might depend on our quest progress. If they've made them, we should get access eventually."

Down halls, up stairs, Maple's head was constantly swiveling— and at last, the guard stopped before a massive doorway.

"Through here. Go on in."

With that, the guard pushed the doors open, letting them see what lay beyond.

It was as wide and long as any boss room, and powerful-looking guards lined both walls. There was a throne at the back, on which sat an old man with a white beard, a crown on his head.

"The king?"

"Sure looks like one. Kinda weird they'd just let anyone in..."

As Maple and Sally whispered, the king called out to them.

"Travelers! You've come at the perfect time."

"See, Sally, there is something going on!"

"Mm-hmm, let's hear what."

"In the near future, our country and the neighboring land will hold a ritual, the results of which will impact the year to come. Visitors to our lands are welcome to join in."

"Aha."

"Is that referencing the event? Oh, the quest updated."

Like Sally said, the quest they'd automatically received updated to the next stage—*Choose your side.*

There was a time limit on it, and even Maple figured out that was when the next event would begin.

"You were bathed in our light upon your arrival; for now, you're in our camp. Naturally, you are free to switch sides. Those are the rules."

So all they had to do was visit the other town, walk under that crystal's light—and they'd be on the other side. They were also told if they belonged to neither camp, they'd be automatically assigned to one. But participating in the fight itself was entirely voluntary.

"This ritual is a demonstration of each nation's power. There is no risk to life or limb; you'll be raiding replica castles created with magic. We expect great things from those who join our side."

In other words, the next event's field would be a duplicate of the current stratum map, and the ultimate goal...toppling the castle at the rear of each side's camp.

They could take advantage of the terrain to attack, sneak stealthily inside, or engage in a frontal assault; lots of options were available to them.

This was a much larger scale than the previous guild wars. It would be difficult to command or coordinate with other guilds during battle—cooperation was easier said than done.

The detailed rules had not yet been revealed, but at least the format and goal were clear.

Players not in either camp likely meant anyone who had yet to reach this stratum. Latecomers would have a distinct advantage— they'd know more about the terrain and facilities.

"If you have questions, come ask. My door is always open."

With that, the guard who showed them into the audience chamber led them back out.

"I urge you to join our camp," the guard said, his back to them. "Their king is strong, but ours is stronger. Though perhaps that's hard to believe if you haven't seen him in action."

Speaking favorably of your own leader was natural enough, but even allowing for that, he seemed to mean it. And this suggested the king himself would take to the field.

"A strong king…"

"Old men are weirdly crazy powerful in games. Who knows what his fighting style is, but I guess we'll find out later."

"True."

Maple was nodding along. As the others shared their views, they reached the castle entrance.

"Preparations for combat have already begun. Outside the gates, look down at the town below. You'll see a large building in front of you. If you wish to help, head there. They have all manner of jobs posted."

"Got it!"

"I guess we go there?"

"Yep. The quest updated, too!"

"He said, 'all manner of jobs,' but I bet that's where this quest starts to branch."

"It seems like NPCs will join the fight, and we might still switch sides. If we complete quests here, will we be strengthening our enemies?"

"Could be, yeah. But let's look at what the jobs are first."

"I hope they're easy…"

"We haven't taken many documented quests like these! I don't know if we can finish them."

"I doubt it'll be a real problem. This is the main event for the stratum, after all. They won't be impossible."

"Good!"

"W-we'll do what we can…"

Mai and Yui had clear strengths and weaknesses, so there were lots of quests they simply couldn't handle. Monsters, they could kill. But if any other abilities were required, they'd quickly run into issues.

"Then let's see what they got!"

"Yeah. And I bet there's tons to do here outside this main quest."

The town was big, and the world outside was even bigger. Given how previous maps had worked, there were likely all kinds of hidden secrets waiting out there.

"Yes—and not just quests!"

"Heh-heh, the more fun, the better."

"Yeah… Is that the building?"

Maple was pointing at a magnificent structure, one so big and tall it stood out even at this distance. Like the rest of the town, it was made of white stone and faced a major road. Several times larger than any structure around, it clearly was divided into several sections within. There was a tower rising from the center of it, with a bell at the top—even as they watched, it started ringing, signaling the time.

"Seems like. Got that landmark vibe, and the location's marked on our quest log."

"Cool. Then let's move, Sally!"

"Yup, yup, watch your step."

With that, they headed back down the long staircase.

After a lengthy walk, they arrived outside their destination. It was bigger than the Guild Homes of the biggest guilds—so big, it could handle all the players who had gathered to take quests.

"Coming through!"

Maple opened the doors and peered in. The space inside was as vast as they'd expected. Walls were covered in job postings, and counters had NPCs waiting behind them.

There were tables and chairs so players could sit and discuss the jobs, and signs showed the way to shops selling food and potions.

There were stairs leading to floors above, making it seem like a massive collaborative Guild Home.

"Wow, it's huge!"

"Those shops in the back might be worth seeing. They want us operating out of this building, after all."

"We'll have to see what's on sale."

"Yep, they're adding new things with every stratum."

"Now, about those quests…"

To avoid jams, it was set up so you could accept quests at both the board and counters. Maple Tree quickly scoped out what was currently available.

"Man, it's like a proper Adventurers Guild!" Chrome said.

Maple and the twins didn't know what he meant.

"Nothing fancy, just—there are places like this in other games."

And that made it easier to figure out next steps.

Sally took Maple with her to browse the postings.

Standing near the boards prompted a pop-up screen filled with quest names. Clicking any of them displayed the full details.

"Wow, there's a lot!"

"We can all find quests that suit our builds. Fighting, gathering...even hauling cargo."

"The main quest that sent us to the castle just says to accept further quests here, so I doubt it matters what we take."

"Yeah, that's likely why there's so much variety."

"We could all take different ones, with our numbers. I want to know more about these quests and what happens after. Especially if there are two towns."

"Then lemme grab one."

"Anything the two of us can do?"

"Hmm...are you seeing anything, Mai?"

They all looked through quests until they found one right for them.

"If you picked anything someone else can manage, do share."

"Let's knock these out!"

They split up, heading for the quest locations.

Maple and Sally had picked the same quest, so they headed to a tall mountain not far from the town. Sheer rock faces, felled trees, water and ice defying gravity—and a trail threading through it all to a series of holes in the side of the mountain.

Clearly, this was a mining path. There were NPCs walking up and down it, hauling glowing crystals from the back.

"The ninth stratum sure has a lot of NPCs."

"Other towns were mostly filled with players!"

There were plenty of structures outside the town walls. This mine was an extension of that. Peering through the teeming crowd, they found a muscular NPC in work clothes barking orders. The quest progress marker hovered over his head.

"Guess we talk to him?"

"Let's try."

As they approached, the man turned and started talking.

"Ah! You took the job? Thanks. This way."

He turned and headed along the cliff face, eventually pointing at the open shafts.

"Some monsters have taken up residence inside. Too many of them, and we can't work the shaft. You know how to fight those things? Take 'em out for us!"

"Will do!"

"Some of them use ice attacks. Don't get yourself turned into an icicle."

"Good to know!"

Once Maple responded enthusiastically, the man headed back downhill. Because monsters were around, this area was devoid of NPCs, but the sounds of their work still echoed in the distance.

"Guess we've gotta get inside. How should we do this?"

"What about riding Syrup and taking them one at a time?"

"Hmm, sounds good. You're getting better at fine control."

Maple summoned her pet turtle, used Psychokinesis to make it hover, and directed it alongside one of the shafts.

"Thanks, Syrup!"

Once inside, Maple put Syrup back in her ring. The shaft itself wasn't wide enough for them to ride the Giganticized turtle around.

"Doesn't seem like a dungeon."

"Nope. Too small... Might be hard for me to fight here."

The ground was hardly even, and it was only just wide enough for them to walk side by side. Sally's combat style was all about mobility, so this curtailed that dramatically.

"Then this one's all me?"

"Yep, go for it."

"You bet!"

This was a simple monster-extermination quest. Kill the target number of monsters, and it was done.

"Martyr's Devotion! Deploy Artillery!"

Maple aimed her cannons forward and took the lead. The narrow passage made it hard for Sally to dodge, but the protective skill kept her safe—they were set on offense and defense.

They walked a bit but didn't find any monsters.

"I'm not seeing any."

"Hmm... I've got my eyes peeled! We're fi—augh!"

"Maple?!"

As Maple focused on the tunnel ahead, she suddenly fell flat on her face. That, at least, wasn't enough to smash her weapons, but it did leave her confused. Sally took her hand and helped her up.

"Watch your feet, too," she said.

"......? Oh! Ice!"

Once she poked at it, it was obvious—and looking closely, the frozen surface *was* reflecting light.

"If you fall during a fight, you'll be wide open. Let's move carefully."

"Yeah! That really got me. I thought I'd been attacked from below!"

Watching their footing, they moved on.

* * *

Sally and Maple were quite far down the shaft now. The ground was still frozen, and now there were icicles dangling from the ceiling.

"Shouldn't be much farther."

"Look out! Above and below."

"Mm-hmm!"

Taking care not to slip and fall again, they moved on—until they saw a floating lump of ice. There was an HP bar above it, and it was generating a blizzard, ice and snow swirling in the air around it. It was clearly moving with purpose; it might have looked like a chunk of ice, but it was more likely a fairy or an elemental. The cold made the icicles above their heads even larger, proving this was the source.

"There it is!"

The monster spotted them, too. The swirling winds grew stronger, knocking the icicles off the ceiling and sending them flying at the girls.

"Use your shield!"

"Okay!"

Always best not to let pointy things hit her body. Attacks that pierced armor generally looked like they would or had skill names that suggested as much.

Using Burning Devour, she swallowed up the icicles, then counterattacked.

"Full Deploy! Commence Assault!"

Maple produced all her guns and took aim at the ice elemental. But when she gave the order, her guns failed to respond—not a single projectile fired.

"Huh? Augh! They're frozen shut!"

There were ice caps on the barrels and icicles dangling from the guns. In game terms, this monster sealed certain types of skills, preventing Maple from attacking.

"Let's figure something out before you run out of Devour... It's pretty slow. Or entirely immobile?"

"True!"

Moving carefully across the slippery floor, Maple made it to the elemental before the rapidly expanding icicles could fall again.

"If you don't move...ha!"

Maple swung her shield hard, smashing it into the lump of ice. Her shield could swallow up any average monster in a single blow, and this elemental proved no exception—it instantly vanished.

They might be on the ninth stratum, but this was an early quest; the monsters weren't meant to be that tough.

"Noice. Keep that up till you're out of uses. Don't wanna see what other attacks they've got."

"Me neither!"

"I'll handle the icicles. I've adjusted to the icy floor; attacks that basic won't be a problem."

Snapping and throwing those icicles was the only attack the monster had attempted. Players might have poor footing, but there was a lengthy delay before the monster could attack a second time. Even with Maple's weapons sealed, this did not pose a real threat. Martyr's Devotion was working just fine, so they were as tanky as ever and should get through this without a struggle.

"Only nine more!"

"I wonder where they are?"

"It's a one-way path, so...deeper in?"

"All right! Let's get 'em!"

With the first monster dispatched, they set off down the mine shaft to clear the quest.

It *was* an early quest, so they made steady progress.

Maple's weapons might be sealed, but the enemies' icy attacks didn't work on her. Sally was batting all the icicles away. Once they got up close, all Maple had to do was swing her shield.

The goal was ten kills—but since she'd used Devour on the first icicle attack, they couldn't dispatch *all* the elementals that way. For the last few, Sally took over the offense, easily taking them down.

"And that's the last one!" Sally said as the ice shattered into light around her dagger.

"Quest clear, Sally!"

"It is the first one we picked—about the difficulty I expected."

"Easy-peasy!"

"It's not a hidden quest; they want everyone clearing it, so they're likely not being too nasty."

"Makes sense."

"You aren't exactly going to be facing boss-class enemies all the time. Not like the top floor in the tower event."

"That was really tough!"

As they made more progress, they'd likely face tougher foes and more complex quests.

Until that happened, they'd just have to clear the quests they found.

"Let's head back. There'll probably be an event once we get out."

"Okay!"

Mindful of their footing, they picked their way back to the entrance, climbed back on Syrup, and flew back to the ground below.

The man who'd led them here was waiting and looked pleased to see them.

"Gosh! You really did the trick! Now we can get back to work. You'll find your reward waiting at the counter in town! Everyone's going to be busy, so I hope you'll help out elsewhere, too!"

"Yup, yup!"

"Time we head to town. I bet the others are finished, too."

The rest of the guild had picked quests of similar difficulty, and it was unlikely they'd really struggled. Some of them might be back already, so the girls left the mines behind.

In town, they headed to the counter to turn in the quest.

A lot of what the ninth stratum had to offer happened here; like their first visit, it was packed with players.

"We just report here?"

"Looks like."

Once they neared the counter, the quest automatically updated, allowing them to turn it in. They tapped the button on the pop-up screens and received materials, gold, and XP in return.

"Whoa!"

"I knew there was a reward for it, but it does feel pretty nice."

"I know, right?"

They'd obtained materials and XP in the mine, too. Getting more from quests meant they could level up faster.

These quests were a key component of the ninth stratum and were clearly designed to encourage players to complete a lot of them.

"The others aren't back yet?"

"We didn't agree to meet here or anything. They could just be exploring."

They'd barely scratched the surface of what the stratum had to offer; there was a lot to learn. Unlike the eighth floor, there were no restrictions; players could spend hours wandering the map.

"What do you think? We could keep taking quests, or we could go out hunting for something more unique."

Focusing on quests would give them a steady reward flow, but nothing as explosive as what you'd get from hidden storylines or dungeons. Still, the ninth stratum was quest-based, and grinding out a bunch might unlock better quests; it was likely worth spending a fair chunk of time on them.

"Hmm...good question..."

While Maple waffled, a familiar face stepped through the door. Maple's and Sally's gear stood out in any crowd, so she spotted them right away.

"Hey, girls. Maple Tree's on this side for now?"

"Lily!"

"Rapid Fire's over here?"

"We're split at the moment. Can't make up our minds without seeing what each has to offer."

Maple Tree had planned to do much the same thing. Rapid Fire had sent members in each direction, gathering intel.

"It seems the event will be based on this map," Wilbert said.

Thus, the more you knew the lay of the land, the bigger your advantage. The larger guilds could dedicate more members to exploring and really exploit that.

"Yeah, it's all about the preparation phase."

All players would be exploring with one eye on the upcoming PvP battles.

"We've been to both sides already. The sooner the better, we thought; hard to make a real decision if you haven't been there personally."

The twin lands had very different terrains. Their guild members would report in, and they could read the boards, but nothing beat firsthand experience.

"Both towns have quest boards; I doubt we'll have time to make much progress if we're trying to play both at once."

"Fair…"

Nobody knew where these quests led, but odds were strong they would give them an advantage in the event itself. Better to make a choice early rather than play both sides and get nothing to show for it.

That was why Lily and Wilbert had hit up both the first day.

"Sally, wanna see the other half ourselves?"

"Okay. Seems like good advice."

They'd been unsure of their next move, so this cleared up that problem, too. They'd have to pick a side eventually, so no time like the present.

"If you discover anything worth knowing, do pass it along."

"Heh-heh-heh, not if we're gonna be on opposite sides."

"Ha-ha, such a pity."

But for now, nothing was set in stone. Sharing info was no different than helping each other clear dungeons on previous floors.

They just had to be mindful of the looming PvP.

"We'll have to party up again someday."

"Okay!"

Wilbert and Lily bobbed their heads and headed farther in. Players were gathering in the corner—presumably other Rapid Fire members reporting in on their discoveries.

"It's time we left town!"

"Let's see what the other side's like."

"It feels like it'll be full of aggressive monsters and traps…"

But no way to be sure until they got there. They'd planned to stay a while on this side, but instead, they headed for the fire and lightning wasteland.

They left behind the green fields studded with water and ice. The flowers thinned, and the forests died away.

At the border between the twin lands, the wild wasteland and the lush forest mingled together, fighting for dominance.

Once through that, the opposite field lay before them.

Tall rocky outcrops, like a forest of stone. Between those, a desert. Lightning and fire were regularly erupting from the rocks; like the floating water and ice, they gave this field a unique atmosphere.

Where creeks had been, molten lava flowed, giving the place a volcanic glow.

"Maybe don't touch those."

"Yep, lava will burn."

Even Maple could not block fixed damage. No matter how high her defense was, it didn't matter if something totally ignored that stat.

They'd have to cross this field to get to town, and naturally, they encountered monsters along the way. As they rounded a rocky outcrop, yard-long lizards slithered out.

"Ha-ha-ha! I got this! Full Deploy!"

Maple brought out her guns and began firing with wild abandon. A barrage of this scale was mostly impossible to dodge, and it tore through lizard after lizard. But this *was* the ninth stratum; that alone wasn't enough to wipe out the pack. The girls were soon surrounded, and the lizards started breathing fire.

"Gonna evac!"

Martyr's Devotion wasn't active, so Sally made an invisible platform in the air to launch herself out of harm's way. Maple just kept firing, letting their flames roast her; her defense was simply too much for them. The lizards had sturdy scales and were on the tanky side, but they couldn't compete. She just stood there in a pillar of fire, generating new weapons as fast as her old ones broke.

Sally landed not far away, watching.

"She's fine…which is weird, but works for us."

Maple's HP bar wasn't budging at all. And the more hits the lizards took, the fewer there were.

Without any means of damaging her, neither their attacks nor their numbers did any good.

"Not even close."

"Plain old fire is nothing!"

"So much for lizards… I wanna know what else is out there."

"…?"

"I mean, we'll be fighting on this map, right? There'll be monsters. If the side we're attacking is full of monsters that give us trouble…that isn't great."

"Oh! Good point!"

"That seal was nasty, but loads of aggressive enemies isn't ideal, either. No good way to handle a random encounter."

"Mm-hmm…right…"

Maple decided to memorize what monsters she saw where. For once, they had early warning on the nature of the event; that meant she had to change her approach to exploration.

"We'll have to keep an eye out for good hiding spots!"

"Yep, harder to get ambushed, easier for us to ambush people. Plus…we don't wanna go running into a dead end filled with lava."

"That would be bad!"

They climbed aboard Syrup, keeping an eye on the monsters below and learning the lay of the land as they headed to town.

Not long after, as the town drew near, they reviewed the monsters they'd spotted.

"Um, big cacti that shoot needles, giant bugs that crawl out of the ground, and fire and lightning versions of the elementals we fought in that mine quest."

"Feels like only the cacti would do piercing damage. We'll have to verify that."

They'd seen the needles flying, and the visual suggested she'd better not risk that attack. She'd quickly snapped her shield up, so the truth eluded them. With that many piercing projectiles, Maple's HP pool likely wouldn't hold out—Indomitable Guardian didn't help much against multi-hit attacks. The other monsters had seemed safe enough, so she'd soaked a hit and made sure their attacks weren't piercing.

As the lizards had indicated, the monsters that appeared on this side were completely different.

"We'll have to take into account our compatibility with the elements and attack patterns involved."

"So much to think about!"

"All the players have more options now, and that means more factors to consider."

When they were at a low level with a handful of skills, they'd only had so many approaches; plenty of things just didn't bear thinking about. That was no longer the case.

"Monsters like these we could handle in the thick of things— but better safe than sorry."

Some were trickier than others, but they were all common field spawns, the kind of enemy you chewed through when grinding XP. Nothing especially challenging about them. Most players capable of reaching this stratum were only going to struggle with bosses.

"We could talk all day, but better to scope out the town."

"True!"

They were already at the town entrance. Walls towered all

around. Through the gates, they could see black stone buildings; where the first town had fountains and ice sculptures, this one had lightning and lava everywhere.

Much more ominous and intimidating than those tranquil white buildings—but they didn't let that stop them.

The first thing they discovered: There was little difference in the facilities available to them. The main road ran from the gate to the castle, and the NPC shops alongside it were in more or less the same locations.

The only real difference—far fewer human NPCs.

Non-humans, however, were plentiful. The NPCs here had animal ears and tails, dragon wings, etc. Very distinctive.

"Aha. I get what vibe they're going for."

"Like the fourth stratum! Or the flying castle!"

"I guess, yeah. They had those dragonewts."

Scoping out the town, they headed up to the castle. The original quest autopaused, and they received a new one, directing them to the throne room.

Each country had its own main quest, and you couldn't have both active.

"So we'll have to pick."

"I guess so!"

The basic procedures were identical. They headed up to the castle, climbing a long flight of stairs.

Outside the castle gates, they found guards with scale-covered faces, exactly like the creatures they'd fought at the flying castle.

Once more, they were led through the halls to see the king. On the way, the dragonewt guard told them a few things about the kingdom and their king.

"The king is super strong! She's in the throne room—but watch your tongues, or you'll get flattened!"

He laughed.

"Wh-what's she like?"

"Definitely sounds more aggressive than the other king."

That king looked more the wizard type. This one sounded more like a melee fighter.

"That would make the water and nature kingdom's ruler better on defense. Though not sure how directly they'll be involved."

Given the size of the player base, it seemed likely hordes would be going at it with fights breaking out everywhere.

No matter how good a player was in hand-to-hand combat, there was a limit to what any one person could do.

But magic might go a long way to covering that weakness.

"Kanade has several grimoires with insane range."

"Yeah… I can't do much unless I'm close, but magic makes up for that!"

Maple's stats also played a factor there; she often couldn't get close enough to her foes and knew just how vital a factor range was.

In time, they reached the throne room. The soldier opened the doors for them, waving them in.

"So big…!"

"Yeah!"

This one was half a room larger than the water/nature kingdom's throne room. Since there was no one in the room but the king herself, it felt even bigger.

"Your Majesty! Guests! Travelers!"

At the soldier's cry, the king stood up. Then she bent her knees—and vaulted all the way over to them. She stopped dead in the air and landed gently.

This close, they got a really good look at her. She was only a bit taller than the girls, with messy black hair a tad longer than Maple's. Her wiry build was distinctly female, but she was covered in hard scales, with sharp claws on her hands and feet, wings on her back, and a large tail.

"Hmm?"

She gave each an appraising look, then nodded, backing off a bit. Her wings and tail vanished in a puff of black light, and her limbs shifted to human ones.

"These look puny, too!"

"You can't judge by appearances! You prove that yourself, Your Majesty!"

"Ha-ha, perhaps I do. This is my kingdom, travelers. You're welcome here!"

They were then given a very similar speech about the upcoming event, picking sides, and the jobs available.

"Oppose us, and I'll show no mercy. If that alarms you, better take our side!"

The king seemed sure of her strength. Her speech concluded, she ordered the soldier to escort them out.

On the way back from the throne room, they shared their impressions.

"……She's quite a character."

"She does seem strong!"

"Going up against her would mean factoring in the way she moves. With those wings, I bet she can fly…but that also means it's easier to predict how she'd fight than the other king."

She definitely seemed like a physical fighter. And the whole dragon theme likely meant she was pretty powerful.

"She's quick, and her human form is rather small—which is a strength."

"You're the best proof of that, Sally."

Maple would struggle to keep up with her.

"If this were just a fight against the king, we'd have an easier time on this side. Your skills are great against AOE spells. I mean, that old man king seems more like a wizard than an infighter."

"True, true."

Still, at this point, it was all conjecture. They needed a lot more info to make any decisions.

For now, they'd met both rulers and scoped out some of the monsters. They'd have to learn more before deciding what to do.

"There's plenty of time until the event begins, so no need to rush things."

"Right!"

They'd only just started exploring the ninth stratum. The real work still lay ahead.

They left the castle, on the hunt for more intel.

---

552 Name: Anonymous Archer
Pick a side!

553 Name: Anonymous Greatsworder
I need more time!
Doesn't seem like either side's got a clear advantage right now.

554 Name: Anonymous Mage
Really?
I only been to the one.

555 Name: Anonymous Greatsworder
The towns themselves are virtually identical.

The skins are unique, but even the shops are all in the same places;
clearly designed to be evenly matched.

556 Name: Anonymous Spear Master
That's how it should be.
If one side was clearly worse everyone would go with the other.

557 Name: Anonymous Mage
I went with the nature side.
Just easier for me.
It's calming.

558 Name: Anonymous Great Shielder
I get that.
That stuff matters when picking a base.

559 Name: Anonymous Greatsworder
But the other king's this loud and proud dragon chick.
Ain't no way a random grandpa can compete.

560 Name: Anonymous Spear Master
The old timer's pretty cool, too!
Just for a different crowd.

561 Name: Anonymous Archer
I know some people switched sides for that alone.
If that's what motivates you, more power to you.

562 Name: Anonymous Greatsworder
Dragon Girl King=goated.

Plus she seems mad strong.

563 Name: Anonymous Great Shielder
I've heard secondhand, but not actually seen her.
Sounds like she can really move.

564 Name: Anonymous Archer
Bows won't be much use against her, so I might as well side with her.

565 Name: Anonymous Greatsworder
The grandpa's threat factor is a black box, but you gotta work with what you know.

566 Name: Anonymous Spear Master
Maple was sighted on the dragon girl side...
Does that mean she's going that way?

567 Name: Anonymous Great Shielder
For now.
Long run, who knows. They're sightseeing and doing their homework.

568 Name: Anonymous Greatsworder
Known threat versus an obvious one.

569 Name: Anonymous Great Shielder
True

570 Name: Anonymous Archer
NPCs a secondary consideration.
Which side will the real last boss take?

571 Name: Anonymous Mage
No shortage of comparable monsters.
They're gonna be with us or against us, so that will be a factor.

572 Name: Anonymous Great Shielder
Too much we don't know.
The event map could keep all the monsters.

573 Name: Anonymous Archer
Oh!
Guess I'd better get more AOE skills.

574 Name: Anonymous Greatsworder
Lots of wide-open space on the border, good for ranged fighters.
Get a bunch of mages and archers there and you can't get close
easily.
Most of you will have AOEs by this point.

575 Name: Anonymous Spear Master
Closer you get to the castles, the easier defense gets. Should
exhaust whoever's going on the attack.
Gotta work close with other players, think about formations.

576 Name: Anonymous Great Shielder
That'd be best, yeah.
You need numbers and teamwork to win.

577 Name: Anonymous Mage
Your guild has a creature who proves that's a lie.

578 Name: Anonymous Spear Master
And she's out there buffing allies.
Angel form.

579 Name: Anonymous Greatsworder
The strongest individuals plus a team up.

580 Name: Anonymous Archer
But the scale here is way bigger than the fourth.
Whichever side has more guilds working together will probably win.
No matter how strong any one player is, they can't be in two places
at once. Get behind them and...

581 Name: Anonymous Spear Master
I don't know other guilds like I know my own.

582 Name: Anonymous Mage
We gotta have talks and shit.

The full details of the event were still unknown; all players were forced to speculate and prepare accordingly.

But it was clear the guilds with the most accurate reads would have a real advantage.

For that reason alone, everyone was out there gathering all the information they could, hoping to bring victory to their doors.

CHAPTER 2

Defense Build and Free Exploration

Having taken a quick look at both sides, Maple decided to stick with the water/nature kingdom for the time being. She went back through the gates, making sure the alliance indicator updated.

The rest of the guild agreed to focus on one side for now, dividing up the research tasks according to their skill sets. Chrome and Kasumi were on combat, Kanade and Iz on towns and items, etc.

From the quests they'd done so far, it didn't seem like anything available was especially difficult. For that reason, Maple Tree decided not to actively pursue them, instead focusing on learning as much as they could to prepare for the upcoming event.

Iz, for instance, was gathering materials and recording the locations of gathering spots.

If the event used this same map, there was value in being able to swiftly acquire supplies.

She'd needed to stock up on ninth-stratum materials anyway, so this killed two birds with one stone.

Otherwise, they were scoping out monster locations and skills, like Maple and Sally had done on their own. Chrome and

Kasumi were exploring, marking terrain suitable for attacking and defending.

Compared to the fourth event, each camp had a lot of ground to cover, with all sorts of terrain in it. Inevitably, there were going to be blind spots; their goal was to eliminate as many as possible.

As for their guild master, Maple?

"Um, they said to explore freely, but…I just can't decide."

She didn't have anything she was specifically after, so she was just sort of wandering aimlessly.

"I guess I just go where the others haven't?"

They were regularly trading messages about where they'd been. As long as she went the other way, she could avoid overlapping research.

Still, her guildmates hadn't issued that instruction so she could fill in the gaps; they were hoping Maple's knack for finding the unexpected would kick in.

That fact was lost on the girl herself, so she was just doing whatever tickled her fancy. Like she always did.

"Syrup, what do you think?"

Her turtle was walking beside her and, shockingly, did not answer.

"All righty then, this way it is."

She'd been told to do whatever she wanted, so she'd followed the standard approach on the ninth stratum and taken a bunch of quests at once while scoping out the terrain.

This time, that brought her to a forest—even from a distance, she could tell it was frozen over. The tall trees were glittering in the light, every branch coated in ice.

She wasn't really in a hurry, so she took her time getting there. Each tree was covered in a thick layer of frost, and she could see through that to the wood within, like it was cryogenically frozen.

"It sure is pretty... Why doesn't it melt?"

She tapped the surface, and the sound echoed. It wasn't melting at all from the heat of her hand; it would likely stay this way.

"Welp, guess I'd better start looking!"

This quest had her gathering rare materials: frozen leaves. Not from the trees all around her, but something more distinctive.

Gathering quests were really Iz's thing, but for good reason, this wasn't a place Iz could safely go alone. She'd been forced to pass on it.

Maple had heard about this from her guildmate and busied herself searching—until that reason showed itself.

"Where could they be?"

The ground was icy, so she had to keep her eyes peeled to avoid slipping.

This was still an early quest, so she didn't have to look all that long.

The ice on the leaf was extra thick, but the leaf itself was a bluish green that really stood out—as promised, Maple spotted it right away.

"It's kinda high up, though."

There wasn't enough room to Giganticize Syrup, so she switched shields.

"It's been a while since I did this!"

She'd found this purple crystal shield in the second event. The skill it came with made a crystal wall grow from the ground.

It was supposed to be defense, but Maple usually used it as something to climb on.

Once the wall was done forming, she clambered up on it and was able to reach the leaf.

"Let's see... Yup, that's the one!"

Now she just had to rinse and repeat until the quest was over.

But a few leaves later, she heard a roar. It was the reason Iz hadn't taken this quest herself.

It was small compared to the one they'd fought at the flying castle, but it was definitely a dragon. Blue scales, broad wingspan, and flying right at her.

"Whoa, there it is!"

Before Maple could do anything, the dragon sprayed the area in water breath.

It caught her by surprise, and she couldn't see a thing, but she didn't take damage.

"Whew!"

Her relief did not last long; the dragon's next attack was a blast of cold air. Maple and the ground around her were still soaking wet, and that water froze, trapping her inside. Devour meant her shield alone was free, but it appeared to be incapable of swallowing the rest of the ice.

"......Uh-oh!"

She was frozen solid, unable to move her arms and legs. The ice was clear enough that she could still see, at least. Maple racked her brain for a way to melt the ice, but then a shadow fell on her.

Another attack. A massive ice clump generated over Maple's head—and dropped on her. Since she was unable to dodge, it scored a direct hit, smashing the ice coating and sending her flying sideways.

"Woo! I'm free!"

Since it didn't hurt at all, she was just delighted to be out of the ice prison. If it did that attack again every time, she wouldn't have to worry about melting anything.

"Deploy Artillery! Commence Assault!"

Returning the favor, she fired her guns at the sky, but the

dragon was a slippery one, and few of her bullets hit. She wasn't getting anywhere.

"This is gonna take ages!"

Maple gave up and started walking away. The fight wasn't her real goal here.

The dragon froze her every now and then, but this wasn't a threat to Maple.

She decided to simply ignore it. Nobody but her could get away with that.

"I won't stay long!" Maple said, and she hastened to find the rest of the leaves.

A while after that, Maple had been blasted by two kinds of breath attacks so many times that there was no unfrozen ground anywhere in the forest. But all it ever did was temporarily inconvenience her.

Time-consuming, to be sure, but fights she couldn't actually lose were Maple's thing.

Soaking every attack, she gathered the leaves she needed and left the frozen forest, satisfied.

"Whew, that was rough! But now I can turn this in."

The quest itself did not require her to slay the dragon. It was always in that forest, so she might have to face it again someday, but she could easily ignore it once more.

For that reason, she turned around at the forest edge to bid it farewell.

But before her eyes was not a frozen forest, nor waves of water and ice breath—but brightly burning flames.

These died down after a minute, and Maple was surprised to see the trees still coated in ice.

"What was that?"

Maple had only encountered the ice dragon, but it wouldn't surprise her if something else here breathed fire. All the other dragons she'd met had been big on fire breath. Water and ice were far from typical.

Still, the info Sally had provided hadn't mentioned anything like that.

"Might be a rare thing!"

Since she'd been told to explore freely, no one would blame her for going back in even though the quest was done.

And so she headed back inside to find the source of the flames.

They'd only been visible for a minute, but the magnitude had been immense. Wondering what could have caused that, Maple found not a monster—but a player.

"Oh, Mii!"

"Maple! You on this quest, too?"

"Yup! I'd just finished up when I saw crazy fire and came back to see if it was something rare."

"Ah-ha-ha. Nope, just me."

"Makes sense. I wondered if that dragon had started breathing fire!"

The stronger the skills one had, the more players started generating boss-size effects. Maple was often mistaken for a monster herself. Largely because a lot of the time, she looked exactly like one.

"My firepower has increased!" Mii said. "I bet even Maple Tree's members don't have anything that can cover such a vast area with a single skill."

"I don't know every skill they've got, but I sure haven't seen any!"

Iz could do something like that, but it required a lot of preparation that took ages. It seemed likely Kanade had a few similar grimoires in his stacks, but those disappeared once he used them.

Damage higher than Maple's Machine God, applied not to a specific point but a whole area, burning everything in range—it really played to Mii's strengths.

"You killed the dragon?"

"No, but it ran away quick. More like I drove it off."

Now she was free to finish the quest. Mii showed Maple the leaves she'd found.

"Nice! I decided it was too tough to fight and just left it alone."

"Wouldn't that be harder?"

"It froze me solid every now and then, but a minute later, it broke me free!"

"I should be surprised, but I'm not…"

If Mii tried to copy that, she'd be forcibly transferred back to town.

Best for each stick to her own play style.

"What's next for you? You're done with the quest, right?"

"I've picked up several others, so I was gonna move on to the next one!"

"Oh? Like what?"

"Um…"

Maple told Mii about the other quests. Since there were only so many kinds, and anyone could accept them, neither was surprised to find a few they both had active.

"If you'd like, wanna team up for a bit? That should make things easier."

"Sounds good!"

"Cool, let's do that. I'll have Ignis give us a ride."

"Sweet!"

And so they soared away to the next location.

"It's so fast!"

"Unlike your Syrup, it was *meant* to fly."

Ignis was a phoenix and had wings. Maple was just using a skill to make her turtle levitate. Since that was hardly an intended mechanic, they weren't exactly winning any races.

"Quite a few players tamed monsters that let them fly. A few members of my guild were so hung up on the feature they only *just* got theirs."

"Well, it is pretty great."

"The height advantage is huge in combat, and ignoring terrain speeds up travel… They're popular for a reason."

"And you can't fly around like this in the real world!"

"Ah-ha-ha, true. That might be part of the appeal."

They were a long way from the days when Maple and Syrup had the skies to themselves. Many players had gained the power of flight.

"And if we're attacking a castle, you can soar right over the walls."

"……!"

Those Flame Empire members who'd held out might well have given themselves a powerful advantage.

Flying monsters *would* let you just ignore the city walls. It was true that players with flying pets were a minority—it was safe to assume the majority would always be on the ground—but they could be a threat wherever defenses were thin.

"Still, that's some serious patience. There was an event on the eighth floor, too!"

"I could never have waited that long."

"Hopefully it pays off for them."

Catching up, they headed toward their destination.

"Is Maple Tree planning on camping over here?"

"I guess so? I think some of us are checking out the other side, gathering info."

"There's stuff to see on both sides. So you haven't made up your minds?"

They could switch as many times as they wanted until the event began. Just because they'd been exploring on the same side didn't mean they'd end up allies in the event itself.

"Have you decided, Mii?"

"We're equally on the fence. Also…we can technically split our guild for this event."

"Really?"

"Yep. I mean, they haven't announced that officially yet. But when you enter the town gates, the crests are added on a player-by-player basis, not guild."

"True…"

"So it should technically be possible for guild members to oppose each other."

Mii was ready to let her guild members pick for themselves.

"Naturally, if they oppose me, I won't let them off easy. I'm the guild master—I can't afford to lose."

"Considering how strong you are, I'm sure you'll be fine."

"All my guild members are really good. I can't rest on my laurels! You think Maple Tree will all stick together?"

"We haven't talked about it, but I bet we will."

"You've got exactly one full party, and your teamwork's polished up."

Front- and back line fighters, unbalanced builds—but they compensated for one another's weaknesses.

You'd have to think hard to find an upside to splitting them up.

"I wonder if we can get on with the other guilds…"

"You won't know till it starts."

"I hope you end up on our side, Mii!"

"Heh-heh, then you'd better think hard about which side I'll choose."

"I'll try!"

"You do that. Oh, almost there. Hang on tight!"

"Will do!"

Mii gave the signal, and Ignis began spiraling toward the ground below.

They'd arrived at a large lake. It was surrounded by a thick forest, but from above, it was impossible to miss.

The tree trunks near the lake had been forcibly snapped, and even Giganticized, Ignis had space to land.

"Thanks, Ignis."

"This the place?"

"Not a great match for my build, so I figured it's better to knock it out while you're with me. And before I forget the trick to fighting them."

Not long after, the monster Mii described showed itself. Big ripples crossed the pond. Lumps of floating water—a hallmark of this floor—emerged, forming multiple pillars linked by countless paths.

Swimming rapidly through these were a bunch of fish, each about twenty inches long.

They'd seen more than enough foes like this on the eighth floor and the event before that.

As a result, the proper response was ingrained in their bodies—a fact that had convinced them both they could clear this quest.

"Martyr's Devotion!"

"Pyre!"

As Maple shored up their defense, Mii unleashed a powerful fire skill from safety. The flames went right through the water, doing massive damage to the fish within.

"Wow!"

"If they're quick, just use an attack so broad they can't escape it. But the water *does* reduce the damage done."

Surviving a hit that hard was expected on the ninth stratum. The fish didn't have much HP left, but they were taking turns, working together to generate a powerful whirlpool.

"Heavy Body!"

The visuals alone suggested it would send them flying, so before it hit them, Maple quickly used a skill that negated knockback.

It was a flashy move, but not piercing, so it couldn't hurt Maple.

And the fact that she'd pulled out the right skill proved she was getting better at gaming.

"This is much easier when I don't have to dodge. Blue Fire!"

Mii was acting as an overpowered stationary cannon, blasting the water with flames. And that drove home how different this fight was from Maple's usual experience.

Where Sally would dart out and rack up damage, Mii wasn't, and that freed up Maple to use skills she usually couldn't.

"Oh! Hydra!"

With that cry, a torrent of poison shot toward the lake. It stained the columns and paths purple, damaging the fish within. With no party members swimming around out there, there was no need to avoid contaminating the field.

"Yikes…"

What she was doing wasn't much different from Mii's approach, but the effects of poison *looked* gnarlier.

The whole school's HP was now steadily draining, leaving them with so little HP that Mii was killing most of them in a single blow.

Once the water was toxic, the fish's speed ceased to matter. Unable to function out of the water, they had nowhere to run.

It might have looked like a furious battle—as fire, poison, and water went everywhere—but in practical terms, it was a one-sided domination.

When they met the quest's target, the water columns vanished, leaving only a quiet lake behind.

"Whew! Thanks, Maple. It's much easier when I can focus on offense."

"If I'd been alone, I'd have been waiting for ages!"

Letting the poison take care of them was easy but time-consuming.

And all the fallen trees meant rough footing; it would have been much harder for Mii to dodge around. Maple's protection simplified everything.

"Partying with you is so different, Mii."

"Really? I suppose... Kanade's spells are pretty different, and Sally doesn't exactly main magic... So that makes sense."

Maple Tree only had eight members, so there were entire roles they didn't cover. And that included the classic magic DPS.

Kanade *could* fill that role, but with Mai and Yui around, it really wasn't necessary.

And Maple's playstyle only compounded that. Maple could negate all incoming attacks, so there was no need to burst damage a foe before it could start to hurt them. They had far less need for speed kills than other guilds.

"That was faster than I imagined."

"You took a lot of quests, Mii?"

"That was the last of the first batch. I imagine there'll be more, but later ones should be more challenging—and take longer."

The quests available now were the easiest the ninth stratum had to offer. And yet these already put players up against enemies that sealed their attacks or attacked from above. Later quests would likely feature even more powerful foes. Given standard difficulty progressions, that was inevitable.

"You've got quests left, Maple?"

"Quite a few! But we're splitting up the quests among our guild members."

"Ah. Maple Tree's members can likely solo most things, unless it's specifically targeting your build's weakness."

"Flame Empire has a lot more members, so we've gotta try and compete on info gathered somehow."

"Fair. That is always important. Marx is better at it than I am..."

"He would be!"

"And events with a base of operations are where he really shines. Doesn't improve his confidence much..."

But previous events had demonstrated just how good he really was. That was why Mii trusted him.

"I often party with Misery, Marx, and Shin; odds are the four of us will be teaming up for this event. If we do end up on the same side of this, you can rely on all of us."

"Okay! Sounds good!"

They hadn't fought together or against each other that many times, but Maple still knew how strong they were. If they'd honed their strengths, they'd be an even greater asset.

"It's been a long time coming, and this is the final prep. I know you've got an ace or two up your sleeve, Maple."

"Um…best I don't say anything!"

"Heh-heh, right you are. That's frightening, but I also can't wait to find out. And be prepared for anything."

"We'll have to get ready ourselves!"

Maple hadn't lasted this long in any previous games, so she'd never had rivals before. Mii was one of her first. When in doubt, Maple just handled it the way Sally did—with a confident grin.

CHAPTER 3

Defense Build and Schemes

While Maple and Mii were doing quests together, Sally was doing a few of her own—but mostly exploring every corner of the stratum.

"They gave us a tough map, but seeing it with your own eyes makes all the difference."

A brief glance at the map showed obvious landmarks: forests, rivers, and lakes.

But these were ballpark sketches; there wasn't much detail. It showed a river but not how wide or deep it was; and unless a cave entrance was visible for miles, it likely wasn't on the map at all.

Worse, there was no info on what monsters were present until you got there.

If there were dangerous foes—like the dragon that kept freezing Maple—you'd want to note that in advance. That would help low-HP/Defense players like Iz, Kanade, and the twins avoid unfortunate accidents.

"If there are no monsters on the event field, great, but..."

They couldn't count on that. Sally was leaving no stone unturned. She was not about to allow a lack of prep to undermine them. Sally's own Defense stats were worse than most level 1 players, so this sort of research benefited her as much as anyone. Her shapeshifting weapon gave her access to a shield now; if she was operating at full power, there were few attacks she couldn't handle.

In other words, this investigation was for when her focus started flagging. Even if her concentration dropped so far she couldn't dodge reflexively, there were cases where knowledge and experience could help her anticipate what she'd need to do.

So Sally always did her homework.

For that reason, quests and levels were secondary to seeing all the monsters and terrain the map had to offer.

"The fire and lightning side sure has a lot more aggressive tricks."

The water and ice side had its share of attacks and traps that immobilized players—as Maple had discovered.

But the other half was all about direct damage.

Sally saw some clear distinctions in the terrain, too. While the water and nature side had lots of chilly places that lowered AGI, the fiery wasteland was prone to jets of lava—and you could just tell it would hurt.

The former would rob players like Sally and Kasumi of their strengths, while the latter put players like Maple and the twins at the risk of instant death from fixed damage.

Which side would they rather invade? Which terrain would work in their favor? There were a lot of factors, and Sally knew they would play a key role in their final decision.

She soon crossed paths with another player recording the terrain.

"Not often I see you solo."

"......? Sally? Hello."

Hinata bobbed her head in greeting.

"Terrain and monster research?"

"Yes. Velvet doesn't really do much of that... O-of course, she's strong enough she doesn't *need* to, but..."

"Fair enough."

Maple was known for skills that seemed unfair, but Velvet's lightning was a match for that, both in power and range. At the same time, she could keep up with Sally's speed and take the fight in close. She was truly top-tier.

"But I think it's better to cover for her. She can be a bit careless."

"I haven't known her long enough to say...but I can see that."

The girl they were talking about had tried to role-play but was not great at keeping up the act. She didn't seem like the type to craft a flawless plan and pull it off without a hitch.

"If she's ready for anything, then we're in trouble."

".........That goes both ways."

Thunder Storm had repeatedly made it clear they were eager to fight Maple Tree. How well prepared they were would influence the outcome of that match.

"But depending on when we pick sides, we might end up working together."

"If that happens...then I hope we can work well together. Velvet might be...disappointed, but that won't make her any less accomplished."

"She's that excited about fighting us?"

"Yes..."

Sally could totally see Velvet's performance being dependent on her mood. Hinata's admission suggested this came out in areas other than her skills—in the details, like deflections and accuracy.

"I don't really wanna face her when she's super hyped."

"Oh?"

Sally saw Velvet and Hinata as natural counters to her own build. They were great with AOEs she couldn't reliably dodge even at peak performance; they'd give her a real run for her money. Players were starting to get skills far more intense than anything the game's bosses threw at you.

"We're doing our own homework. But I'm sure you've looked up as many of our skills as you can."

"......You've certainly made an impact, so...we know things."

Maple tore up the battlefield in every event and was a fixture in the highlight reels. No one who'd made it to the ninth stratum was unaware she could turn into a monster or sprout a ton of artillery.

"The downside of fame."

In the previous PvP event, she hadn't been all that well-known—and they'd been able to turn that to their advantage. That was no longer the case. They'd have to prevail despite the opposition's plans.

"There's a lot less info about your skills than Maple's, Sally."

"Glad to hear it. I'm playing my cards right."

Sally had always been able to dodge things that weren't supposed to be avoidable, which made her less dependent on her skills and better at keeping them secret.

"Well, let's agree to regret nothing."

"That's...one way to put it."

Hinata clearly had her own thoughts on the subject, and Sally assumed that's why she was out here investigating. But this reaction suggested she'd misread things.

"............"

Hinata nodded to herself, making up her mind, then leaned in to whisper. What she said made Sally's eyes go wide and give her a searching look.

"......Huh, you seemed like the quiet type, but I'm revising my assumptions fast. Velvet knows about this?"

"Um, I've mentioned it."

"Sure it won't disappoint her?"

"Maybe, but it'll put us one step closer to victory. I've helped her get her groove back before...and it'll help pay back our guild members for their efforts."

"I see."

"If she gives it enough thought...I think she'll see it's not all bad."

"........."

"If you're so inclined, just send a message. To me or Velvet."

With that, Hinata bowed her head and walked away. Sally stood still for a long minute.

"She wants me to side with them...?"

Sally hadn't planned on *that*. But she couldn't rule out the idea altogether—so perhaps part of her was tempted. After all, there hadn't been any real PvP since the fourth event.

When would the next one be? It could be several months off.

"......"

And that left Sally indecisive.

Meanwhile, Maple and Mii were still doing quests together.

Mii had some time on her hands, so she'd offered to help Maple make quick work of her slate. Maple had agreed, and the OP offense and OP defense combo was literally incinerating monsters everywhere.

Ignis's mobility—plus DPS Maple could never manage on her own—let them burn through the rest of her quest log.

Once they'd finished, they headed back to town to turn everything in.

"A quick trip back!"

"Compared to Syrup, yeah. And faster than Atrocity, I think?"

"Probably!"

Atrocity was certainly faster than Maple's other forms of transportation, but the stats that skin gave her didn't grow. Ignis was a bird, so it had high AGI to begin with; and that was only increasing as it leveled up.

Mii instructed the phoenix to land at the entrance and put it back in her ring. They headed through the gates together.

"You seen much of town?"

"Not really! It's huge, and there's two of them."

"They've got cannons on the walls around town. And guards stationed all over, not just the castle."

"Think we'll use those cannons?"

"In the event? Good question. They had shells, so if we carry them to the cannons, we might be able to fire them."

If they had anti-air weapons anyone could use, then flight might not be the safest option. Better to assume you'd need a pet monster with high mobility and have lots of practice riding it.

"Kanade's tasked with checking out the towns, so I'll ask him later."

"Good idea. You can always check anything interesting yourself later."

"Yeah! I'll do that!"

After walking and talking for a while, they reached the quest hub. Once they'd turned in their respective quests, they noticed the next difficulty level had been added. They knew these monsters would be stronger—and the locations specified weren't plains and forests but mountains, ravines, and deep inside caves. Terrain that restricted players' options.

"Definitely harder."

"Indeed they are."

With other players now around them, Mii had gone back to Flame Empress mode. It took Maple a second to catch on.

"Oh! Right. Uh…do you have plans, Mii?"

"I'm afraid this is as far as I can join you today. I look forward to fighting by your side again."

"Okay! Same here!"

Maple beamed, and Mii smirked. Then they went their separate ways. Their team-up had been very ad hoc, but they had a good idea of each other's core abilities, so they'd made efficient progress.

Mii accepted a bunch more quests for when she next had time, but she left Maple behind, headed off to other plans.

"What should I do…?"

She could move on to the new quests, but they'd just been talking about the town—she could look around here, too.

After some thought, she decided she'd reached a quest milestone, and it was time for a new approach.

"I wanna keep up with both!"

Not just wandering the town but also doing some real exploration in the fiery wasteland.

Maple Tree were currently focused on the watery nature kingdom. If Maple took some quests on the other side, she'd be the first in line.

"I'm gonna play a while longer!"

So instead of taking new quests, she headed out of town.

*   *   *

Outside, Maple boarded Syrup and bobbed off slowly across the sky. The plains around the town didn't have many flying monsters, so her voyage was a pleasant one.

"Sure is a nice view from up here."

That was always true in high places, but this view was extra nice because the land below was so flat.

All this open space around the town made it hard to attack or defend. They'd used a lot of surprise attacks in the fourth event, but that would be hard to pull off here, where everyone could see for miles.

The battles outside town would definitely be determined by numbers. For that reason, Maple turned her attention in either direction.

The farther you got from the town entrance, the more the landscape varied. The frozen forest Maple had visited earlier, places that gave you automatic debuffs (according to Sally)—lots of tricky terrain.

"The way Sally thinks...we'll be in those areas, not the plain outside."

Based on prior event experience, Maple tried to figure out how she'd attack. She was the only Maple Tree member with flight options. For that reason, she felt sure there'd be things only she could see.

"There are flying monsters over there, so I'd better steer clear... but this way looks fine!"

What else did she need to look out for? She ran through her previous experiences.

"Oh! The wind!"

Maple had been caught in a sudden gale on the third stratum that yanked her right off Syrup.

Visible threats weren't the only dangers—powerful winds were a good example.

"Hnggg...well, looking alone won't tell me much. Okay!"

She decided to ride Syrup around and flew off to the other town, taking it upon herself to explore the skies and help Sally out that way.

Even in unknown territory, with Indomitable Guardian and Atrocity, it would take some doing to bring Maple down.

Her own lack of mobility was a sore spot, but the rest of her abilities made up for most risks she was likely to run into while scouting. She was a good candidate for exploring unknown territory.

Adding further aerial exploration to her to-do list, Maple continued toward the other town atop Syrup.

Inside, she hurried to take some quests.

"I wonder if this place has cannons like the ones Mii mentioned?"

She felt like they'd be evenly matched on that front, but it couldn't hurt to see it for herself. For that reason, she followed the walls around the town.

Mii had made it sound like there was a staircase leading up somewhere.

"That looks hot...but maybe isn't?"

There was molten lava running through the town. While taking in those sights, she soon found the stairs she was looking for.

"There we go!"

She began the long climb to the top of the wall. The summit had walls on either side, with chest-high gaps in them; pointed through these were the cannons Mii had described.

"So they stick the tips through these holes to shoot them?"

Both towns faced an open area with nowhere to hide. She wasn't sure how powerful these cannons were, but attacks from this high up had to count for something. Most players had ranged attacks, so they could form ranks on these parapets, slinging spells and arrows and chewing up most forces on their approach.

Maple could throw out her poisons and fire her guns from up here, and the instant-death effect from Bug Urn Curse would do some major damage.

Her build was always great against incoming hordes.

"Oh! There are the shells! Can we use those?"

Maple approached the pile and discovered she could use Gathering here. Naturally, this gave her a cannon shell; she could hold a maximum of three.

It was impossible to treat them like potions and use Gathering inventory with them to burn through as needed, but if several people went back and forth, they should be able to keep the cannons firing near constantly.

"Lemme try it once!"

She moved to the cannon and clicked on the shell. This automatically loaded the cannon; there was a *boom*, and the shell shot out across the field.

"Wow! But would that hit anything?"

In PvP, the main targets would be players. These cannons were way less precise than the Machine God weapons she usually worked with; Maple figured she lacked the finesse to actually aim them.

"Guess I'll just remember they're here. Iz or Sally might make better use of them."

There were lots of cannons, and it didn't seem like there was much variation in power or effect. If they were all firing, that might be a threat, but they'd have to wait until the event itself to find out.

At this point, Maple turned to head back the way she'd come, but she bumped into someone else on the stairs.

"Oh, Frederica!"

"Hmm? Ah, 'sup, Maple? You alone?"

"The others are all out in the field somewhere. I'm exploring solo!"

"Aha. You know, I barely ever run into you. Even though your gear and skills stand out a lot … What do you usually get up to?"

"Uh…I dunno, I just wander around the map. Normal stuff."

"Maple Tree's definition of normal is super sus."

"That's not fair!"

"Heh-heh-heh, but it is."

Given the number of freakish skills Maple Tree members had, most would agree they were anything but normal.

"You here to scout things out, Frederica?"

"Yup, yup. I'm all about backline support and intel!"

She glanced around the top of the wall.

"My buffs…would only reach so far. With our numbers, clumping up…even with AOEs…"

During the raids, Frederica's seemingly bottomless MP pool and sheer quantity of AOE buff skills had proven to be a valuable asset.

But she didn't have anything like the durability of a heavily armored frontline player; she'd prefer to operate from the relative safety of a wall.

Still, there was a limit to how far her skills could reach, and she had to consider the needs of her allies. It paid to examine the pros and cons with brutal pragmatism. She wasn't like Maple; she couldn't exactly wade out into the fray and expect to survive.

"You're on this side, then?" Maple asked.

"Hmm? Well, for now. We haven't made a final decision. Maple, what're you thinking?"

"I'm the only one here right now. We split up to explore!"

"Yeah, you got so few members…"

The Order of the Holy Sword was a vast company, so taking the same approach would inevitably give them far more information.

Sally was adept at gathering intel, but she couldn't cover as much ground as ten other players. The advantage of numbers was not easily overcome.

"No clue what the final standings will be, but Pain is leaning toward putting the whole guild on one side or the other."

"He is?"

"That puts victory closer, right? And I'm not about to oppose him on this one."

Frederica didn't see much difference between the two countries. In which case, she was better off being in the same camp as Pain, Drag, and Dread.

"Gotta back the winning horse!"

"The Order is super strong…"

"You know it. So—your guild may be small, but you're all top of the game. Guild Master of Maple Tree, may we parley?"

"Er, what?"

"I mean talk inside our Guild Home."

"Huh…"

Maple hadn't expected this invitation, but she saw no reason to turn it down. She agreed and followed Frederica away.

Trudging after Frederica to the Order of the Holy Sword's Guild Home, Maple looked a bit tense.

"What's wrong, Maple?"

"Oh, nothing. Just…nerves."

Maple had never been to another guild's home before. Frederica had frequently popped in on theirs, and plenty of other players had visited to ask Iz for help, but she'd never had a reason to call on anyone herself.

"Nothing to be nervous about! You're Maple Tree's boss! Act like it!"

"Huh? L-like this?"

Maple tried to put on her best boss face. Frederica nodded approvingly.

"That's more like it! It's not a big deal."

Soon enough, they were outside the Order's Guild Home. They were one of the biggest guilds in the game so it wasn't surprising that their home was as big as this stratum's quest hubs. It was a four-story building that looked like it went pretty far back.

"It's huge!"

"Ha-ha! We're on a totally different scale from your crowd, so we need the space."

"Wow! It's like a mansion!"

"I know, right?"

As Frederica basked in Maple's reaction, a new voice called out to them.

"You look pretty satisfied with yourself."

"Draaaag! Lemme have this one! It's my guild, too!"

"True enough. And that's not a face we see here often."

"Exactly! I bumped into her, so I brought her along."

"This mean what I think it means?"

"Yup. I know what I said, but if we leave this to Pain, we'll end up fighting whoever's stronger."

"He's levelheaded, but he likes a challenge."

Maple wasn't fully following their conversation, but Drag broke off there, figuring they shouldn't chat while standing around in the street.

"Frederica's got this, so I'm outta here."

"Yup, leave it to me."

"Maple, feel free to check out anything that catches your eye. But be aware you might get some stares yourself."

This was not her guild—and she was *Maple*.

"Okay!" Maple said cheerily.

Drag wiggled his fingers good-bye and vanished into the Guild Home.

"Let's go in ourselves. This way. You can look around once we're done talking."

"Sure thing!"

And thus, Maple finally set foot inside the lair of the Order of the Holy Sword.

Maple followed Frederica through the interior, head swiveling.

"It's just a Guild Home, so the basic facilities are the same. Like yours, but bigger."

"Yeah…"

"The top two floors are individual rooms…but you can look around the first two floors."

"Got it!"

But all that was *after* business. Frederica soon took them to a door, and she knocked.

"Coming in!"

"Uh, hiii…"

They stepped inside and found Pain sitting there. He looked surprised by the unexpected visitor.

"Frederica, what's this…?"

"You remember what I said! Final decision's yours, but if we hold talks early, it'll make my life easier."

"I see… Very well. Maple, thank you for joining us on short notice. Have a seat anywhere."

"Okay!"

Maple plopped down on the couch. Frederica joined Pain across the table from their guest.

"I'm sure Frederica's sudden invitation caught you off guard. But we'd like to discuss the upcoming event."

"Really?"

"Yes, with two camps in opposition, everyone—but especially the largest guilds—are carefully eyeing the standings, wondering when to pick a side."

Sally had pretty much said the same thing. Which guilds wound up on which side would make all the difference.

"With that in mind, the Order is quietly recruiting. That's why Frederica brought you here."

In other words, he wanted Maple Tree on the same side as the Order.

"So we'd be teaming up…?"

"No one doubts Maple Tree's abilities. You'd be a fearsome opponent and a stalwart ally."

"You say that, but part of you was hoping for a rematch, right?" Frederica teased.

Pain winced. "True, opportunities like this are few and far between. You got us good in the fourth event…but I'm also a guild master. I've got an obligation to lead my people to victory."

He was prioritizing the needs of his guild over his personal feelings. He led one of the largest guilds in the game—coupled with the decision to place them all on the same side, it was obvious he'd put a lot of thought into this.

"I'd love to beat Sally, myself!" Frederica chirped.

"Ha-ha, I've heard you often duel her."

"That's its own thing. I want a victory on the public record, too!"

"Don't we all? Sorry, we're getting sidetracked. I'm not expecting an answer here and now. Consult with your members. But if you're willing to side with us, please let us know."

"Will do!"

"You always get right to the point, Pain! Nothing else you wanna say? I mean, we got Maple right here in our house."

"Y-yeah? I suppose…um…we could talk about…"

"Oh, can I ask a question?"

"Hmm? Certainly. I'll try and come up with something myself."

"You're both so stiff!"

"A-are we?"

"We are?"

"Yes!"

Frederica alone was her usual self, and that helped keep the conversation flowing.

Once the conversation died down, Pain touched on the main topic again.

"I'd appreciate it if you'd seriously consider our offer."

"Okay! I'll bring it up with the others."

"C'mon, Maple. I'll show you around!"

"Thanks!"

Not long after they left, Dread came in.

"Frederica brought Maple by?"

"Yes. Is word spreading?"

"Her armor's distinctive. The other guild members tipped me off. Anything come of it? I'm all ears."

"I proposed an alliance. That's the swiftest path to victory."

"……Shocking. Figured you were hell-bent on a rematch."

"Ha-ha-ha. Frederica said the same thing. But the scale of this event is far beyond your standard PvP. We're doing what we can to ensure we can win with the Order's power alone, but…that's a tall order. If I think of the guild, I can't afford to be preoccupied with my personal desires."

"I get that. Pain—you've become a guild master."

"But of course. I shall lead you to victory."

Victory for the entire guild. That was the only thing on anyone's mind as the Order of the Holy Sword readied themselves for the coming battle.

◆□◆□◆□◆□◆

On a later date, Maple was in her Guild Home, thinking hard.

"What should we do?"

Lately, all she could think about was how Maple Tree should approach this event.

Mii said Flame Empire were letting their members pick either side, while the Order insisted on keeping everyone in the same camp. Pain had already invited them to an alliance, and given how many powerhouse players Maple Tree had, they might get similar invites down the line.

She could discuss this with her members, but Maple was the guild master. The final decision would be hers.

"I've gotta make a choice before it starts!"

She left the Guild Home to clear some more quests while she mulled it over.

Unlike the other members, she was on the fiery wasteland side—so still running solo.

"C'mon, Syrup! Let's fly around!"

Maple had her turtle Giganticize and climbed onto its back. They flew off toward a vast forest of trees with black leaves.

"From up here, I can't see the ground at all!"

The branches stretched out far longer than the average forest. It was like a carpet of black leaves.

Inside the forest, it must have been as dark as night.

"Anywhere I can actually get down?"

The quest led her to the center of the forest, but she didn't see anywhere Syrup could land. She could undoubtedly reach her destination starting from the forest entrance, but that would take far more time than this quest deserved.

"If I drop as low as I can, I guess it'll be okay?"

Maple had Syrup hover just above the trees, stood up, and then put the turtle back in her ring.

Since her ride vanished, Maple plummeted straight down through the black-leaved trees and into the forest below.

After a ton of rustling, she landed in a heap on the ground.

"Whew! I made it through. Upsy-daisy!"

Maple scrambled to her feet and looked around. She was right—the forest interior was pitch-black. There were no lanterns anywhere, and she was far from the forest edge, so she couldn't even make out where the tree trunks were.

"Martyr's Devotion! Predators!"

There wasn't much room between the trees, so Machine God's bulk would be a liability here. Her Predators were more flexible and would attack enemies Maple hadn't noticed. Martyr's Devotion kept them safe and also lit up the area. She was set.

The glowing circle provided far better illumination than any headlight.

There was no risk of her accidentally walking headlong into a tree.

"No one nearby... Guess I'll give this a whirl."

Maple pulled up her screen and changed her gear, equipping Lost Legacy.

A black cube with blue patterns on it hovered nearby and began following her around.

"Okay...I'm ready!"

She headed out...and soon found her quest's target.

It was a shadow, stretching and warping like it was made of slime. Part of the body shifted into the shape of a sword, stabbing at Maple.

As it came from in front of her, Maple got her shield up, but she hadn't realized she was surrounded, and a similar attack came from behind her.

Maple couldn't react to stuff like this in time, but Predators could. They targeted anything in their territory, chomping down on the shadow sword and swallowing it.

"Whoa! Behind me?! Thanks! I had no idea!"

Praising her Predators, Maple focused on the foe in front of her. As long as she had Devour uses left, attacks from the front were pointless.

Not only did they not hit Maple—her blocks were a powerful counter that engulfed anything.

Maple fought for a while, patiently waiting for Lost Legacy's energy gauge to fill.

"Is that enough? Okay, Ancient Weapon!"

The moment Maple called the skill name, the cube stopped hovering. It split into a number of smaller cubes and spread out around her.

The cubes released tiny blue flames, like sparks—but an instant later, they extended into strands of blue light, like the bars of a cage.

They went right through any monsters in their paths and did residual damage to any monsters nearby.

"Wow! Nothing can get close!"

Getting to her would require navigating a web of lasers. These monsters were no pushovers, so one hit wasn't taking them out. But they took a solid amount of damage on the way in, and that put them at a huge disadvantage.

And if they did get through, they were simply torn apart by *her* monsters.

"Before this runs out…Saturating Chaos!"

Maple backed up her Predators. Ancient Weapon didn't hurt *her*, so she could fire long-ranged attacks through it while remaining safely inside the laser cage.

Few things could get close, and if they did, she was too tanky. No trash mobs had what it took to penetrate her offense or her defense.

"Whew. I can't use it when it counts if I don't practice…so best to use it when I won't be spotted!"

Ancient Weapon offered more than the laser cage. It also had a Gatling gun that was good for suppressing fire, plus a long-range sniper mode.

Activating these required energy—a dedicated resource—and this steadily declined over time. If she wasn't actively trying to use the skill, she'd never get a chance.

Many of Maple's skills had damage that didn't grow with her stats but were *rare*, so the starting DPS was quite high. If she attacked with any precision, she'd tear through trash mobs before she could expend the energy gauge.

That's why she'd limited her offense to Predators and Devour.

With this pack of monsters down, Maple headed deeper into

the woods. This quest involved cleansing the area of shadows—it would take more than ten or twenty before she was done.

"What should I try next?"

Maple had acquired a number of skills since the fourth event. But her defense was so absurd the monsters just couldn't keep up; as long as she fought at all, they'd go down before she did. For that reason, she was mostly getting by with the same skills she'd used in the past.

That would likely not hold true when fighting players. The whole server knew Maple's weaknesses, and everyone was familiar with her flashy moves.

Which meant the key to victory lay in her newer skills.

It was hard to prepare for the unknown. If Maple wanted to take full advantage of her new acquisitions and do real damage to anyone who made the wrong call, she needed to know her own skills in and out.

First, Ancient Weapon. Then Twisted Resurrection. Two big skills—but Maple hadn't played many games before this one. Despite everything Sally had taught her, she was nearing the limits of her capacity.

"So I'd better take my time!"

The fact that she stayed positive was a sign of how much she'd grown. For a while, the forest filled with laser lights and the screams of dying monsters.

While Maple was trying out the other land, the rest of Maple Tree had scoured the water and nature kingdom for information, and they were now talking about sending a few of their members across the divide.

"Sally's been focused on the monster guide, so we oughtta help with terrain."

"Yes. Maple says the quests themselves aren't noticeably different, so we'd better look at the map."

"Ideally, we'll find some hidden areas only we know about. Strong positions to retreat to even if we get ambushed."

"It'll be huge if we find them."

"So we just keep poking around?"

"W-we'll try and find some hidden areas!"

"The way the previous maps worked, hidden areas aren't *just* hidden; they'll also have stronger monsters. Explore with caution."

"So we're gonna stick with the divide-and-conquer approach. Can't do much if we haven't found it yet."

"Sounds good. All of us together, we can clear out anything. But we can't do that if we don't know where to go."

Hidden areas wouldn't be worthy of the name if they were right where everyone expected them to be. Discovering these locations required close observation and more than a little luck.

"If you stumble across any new materials, I'd appreciate you bringing back a heap."

"......You've barely left your workshop since we got here. Whatcha making?"

"No spoilers. I'll share when the event's closer."

"......Curious."

"I bet it's amazing, Mai!"

Iz could make things other players couldn't, so until she was ready to show off, even top players like Chrome and Kasumi couldn't begin to predict what surprises she had ins store for them.

But everything she'd made had proven useful, so they knew her efforts would pay off.

"Do quests as you go and back up Sally's research!" Chrome summed up.

Everyone nodded, then headed out to the field—Maple Tree was prepping for the event in their own way.

---

623 Name: Anonymous Greatsworder
Alliances forming everywhere.

624 Name: Anonymous Spear Master
Some places making a splash about it, others keep it on the DL...what if too many end up on the same side?

625 Name: Anonymous Mage
I bet they either give the smaller side a boost or cap the other.

626 Name: Anonymous Archer
These alliances are entirely player-driven.
I bet they do cap the sides.

627 Name: Anonymous Great Shielder
Definitely not random, though.
Maybe there's a lottery for the overflow?

628 Name: Anonymous Greatsworder
All we can do is slow and steady prep, increase what we can handle.
With the scale and style of the event I assume it's time accelerated, but there may be a limitation on deaths like the fourth one.

629 Name: Anonymous Spear Master
Would make sense, yeah.
If they just keep coming back like zombies, nothing'll ever resolve.

630 Name: Anonymous Archer
You all doing quests?

631 Name: Anonymous Great Shielder
Some.

632 Name: Anonymous Mage
You can do quests whenever, but there's only so much time before the event.
Gotta learn the map.

633 Name: Anonymous Greatsworder
There's places out there that'll be real nasty if someone sticks a trap in 'em.
If you don't wanna die, you gotta learn to avoid that.

634 Name: Anonymous Archer
Lots of real gnarly spots, yeah.
Like they were specifically designed to be key locations on offense or defense.

635 Name: Anonymous Mage
Terrain has always been the strongest defense, historically.

636 Name: Anonymous Spear Master
You hear about the laser forest?

637 Name: Anonymous Greatsworder
Already don't believe it.

638 Name: Anonymous Spear Master
Black leaves, no light gets in.
But blue lasers shoot out through the branches.

639 Name: Anonymous Archer
I went there for a quest, but it wasn't like that?

640 Name: Anonymous Greatsworder
Monsters dwell in the forest depths, then?

641 Name: Anonymous Great Shielder
Wonder what it could be...

642 Name: Anonymous Mage
The monsters weren't that bad, so I figured it would be good for
ambushes, but if there's an unidentified life-form shooting lasers in
there...

643 Name: Anonymous Greatsworder
Don't wanna try until we know more.
Spear Master, go let one hit you, confirm the damage.

644 Name: Anonymous Spear Master
Hell no.

645 Name: Anonymous Great Shielder
I'm hard to kill. I could take a look.
Doubt it would be instant death.

646 Name: Anonymous Archer
If it is, then only Maple could risk it.

647 Name: Anonymous Greatsworder
If Maple can soak it but it can kill a normal tank, Maple Tree could just hole up in there and call it.

648 Name: Anonymous Great Shielder
Yup.

None of them knew that the girl they thought could soak these lasers…was the source of them.

CHAPTER 4

Defense Build and Strategy Sessions

More time passed, and players were making headway on the available quests. Those provided a clear structure. All these players questing meant locations the quests didn't take you to tended to be left alone—compared to previous floors, at least.

For that reason, a survey of the field showed many areas where no information had been posted.

At this rate, it could be some time before their search for hidden areas paid off.

Meanwhile, Maple was still following her whims, going where she wanted when she wanted. Today, she was standing just outside town, looking over her map, wondering where to go.

Sally had been ignoring quests entirely in favor of mapping the stratum, and the rest of the guild was focusing on their own things—once again, Maple was running solo.

This was *also* because her guild had decided that would work in her favor.

"Where to this time?"

She'd been doing quests as she went, but she had spent a lot of time flying around the ninth stratum and had mostly checked out anything that showed up on the map that caught her eye. Naturally, that was a far cry from having checked out *everything*, and revisiting locations was always an option—but she'd prefer to go somewhere new.

Unexplored locations were guaranteed to offer new discoveries. There was no chance of her search coming up empty.

As she considered which unexplored location to visit, someone called out to her.

"Maple! Whatcha standing around for? Whassup?"

"Oh, Velvet! No Hinata?"

"She's, like, scouting the map."

"Ah, same for Sally. What's your plan?"

"That totally ain't my thing, so I'm grinding levels and exploring the untouched areas."

"Ah-ha-ha, you and me are on the same page."

"That why you got your map open?"

"Yeah, just wondering where to go. You got a destination picked out?"

"I did, but where were you thinking about, Maple?"

Maple readily pointed out the places she'd been eyeing.

"This one's, like, on both our lists! Wanna team up?"

"Sure! Great! Syrup ride?"

"Heh-heh-heh, I know something *faster*."

"You do? Is it your pet monster?"

"*Bzzt*, wrongo!"

They had to be partied up for it to work, so first Maple and Velvet partied up.

"Here goes! Spark Impetus!"

Electricity coursed over both their forms, sparks crackling. What did this do? Well, Maple had already seen Mii use Flare Impetus, so she had a pretty good idea.

"Now just run!"

"Really?"

"You got this!"

Maple ran off as fast as she could. She wasn't even comparable to how fast Sally, Kasumi, or Velvet could go, but the buff made her faster than players like Chrome or Kanade, who didn't really emphasize movement.

"Wow! I'm sooo fast!"

"This'll speed up pretty much anyone!"

This would definitely get them to their destination faster than Syrup could.

"I haven't really run anywhere before!"

"You're really enjoying this, huh?"

"Onward!"

"You bet! Oh, watch out for when it runs out. Miss that, and you'll, like, fall on your face 'cause you're suddenly so damn slow."

"Good to know!"

Racing about the fields made Maple feel like Sally. On newly fleet feet, they sped to their destination. Velvet had to slow herself down a bit to match Maple's pace, but they ran together.

"Kinda weird seeing you run, Maple!"

"If I wanna run, I normally have to use Atrocity. If I blow up my weapons, I can move quick, but that's not really *running*."

Maple rarely went anywhere in her default form. She either rode Syrup or took advantage of the movement options Sally supplied. Machine God and Atrocity made her fast, but those were both meant for combat.

Since her AGI was stuck at zero, any items or skills that would buff that stat did nothing for her. Spark Impetus worked like Atrocity and increased the stat without taking the base value into account. That was why it successfully sped Maple up.

Charges, lightning bolts, and tearing up the battlefield weren't all Velvet could do; she always had support skills like Spark Impetus. Hinata's name was synonymous with support and interference skills, but that didn't mean Velvet had none of her own.

If she had more than just this speed boost, then she was likely as big a threat in group combat as she was in a one-on-one.

"Do you have more skills like this?"

Sally might have reached that conclusion on her own, but Maple didn't think it through. Her question stemmed from pure curiosity.

"Mwa-ha-ha!" Velvet said. "Like I'd tell you that!"

"Oh! Right, fair."

"You'll find out in this next event!"

The way she talked sure made it sound like she did, but until she actually used them, there was no way of telling.

"What about you, Maple? We've fought together a few times, but I didn't see any new skills."

Each time, Maple had used powerful skills like Devour, but always the same ones. Sally had advised her to stick to avoiding anything else, but she was also just partying up with players who were strong in their own right.

If she was with Mii or Velvet, Maple didn't really *need* Machine God. Maple joining the offense did not really speed up the outcome. Paired with high DPS, Maple's role reverted to being a traditional tank.

Why use new skills when she could just pop Martyr's Devotion and do fine?

So Maple cheerily yelled, "That's a secret!"

And they ran on toward their destination.

"Whew! I've never run that far!"

Their feet had taken them to a stretch of uneven ground

punctuated by tall, jagged rocks. Both the rocks and ground were covered in scorch marks, sooty remnants of attacks from something lurking within a cave.

Standing at the entrance, Maple peered in—and a bright light arced overhead, illuminating the vicinity.

"Whoa!"

"Just lightning! That's not, like, gonna hurt *you*, right?"

Velvet was aware of Maple's defense. But this bolt was so powerful she couldn't help but ask.

"I dunno… I feel like lightning usually doesn't ignore defense, but…"

She'd have to take a hit to find out. Indomitable Guardian would likely prevent her from accidentally dying here.

Some of these rock spikes were working like lightning rods. Exploring the area meant identifying these safe areas and moving swiftly between them when they could.

You know, for regular players.

"Martyr's Devotion!"

With Maple's skill keeping Velvet safe, they steeled their nerves and marched forward. There was a flash above, the bolt momentarily blinding them.

But only for an instant. When the light faded, Maple was standing there perfectly unharmed.

"We're good!"

"Rad! Now we can waltz through."

If Velvet stayed in the glowing circle, she took no damage. Unless Maple got hit by a knockback strike and was flung away, at least—and that wasn't really what lightning did.

"The fifth stratum also had a crazy lightning storm…but this might be worse!"

"I use the stuff myself, but I can't match this!"

If Velvet ever managed to bring the thunder this hard, no one would ever get close to her again.

She was currently so good that only Sally could actually dodge her attacks, so arguably, she was way past broken.

"Firing this fast would be damn strong, though!"

"Do your skills level up?"

"Don't seem like it."

Velvet had been maining lightning for a while. And her play style was all about combat; it made sense that she'd have leveled all skills as far as they could go.

With lightning bouncing off them, they walked on—until they found the monsters they were looking for.

These were crackling electric spheres, maybe twenty inches in diameter. Whatever their nature, seeing them flit about between the rocks ahead looked a lot like fireflies.

"That's them!"

"Okay! Full Deploy!"

Maple generated her weapons and fired them all at the monsters.

An attack that excelled in speed and range, delivered from outside their aggro range—very one-sided.

The monsters spotted her barrage too late. The way they bobbed along proved they weren't exactly nimble and could not escape the attack's range.

They'd never looked like they had high HP pools, and Maple had figured she could take them out quick, but even when the bullets scored a direct hit, that just generated sparks, and they passed right on through.

This did not seem to do any damage. Maple had encountered monsters that negated her attacks before.

"Urgh, no use…"

"Then this is all me! Not a great matchup, mind you. Thunder God Advent!"

Velvet began generating far more electricity than the monsters did. Not about to be outdone, they started firing forking bolts back at the girls. Their speed and range were every bit as great as Maple's artillery—tough to dodge.

"I got this!"

Maple just stood stock-still, nullifying all the bolts. Not a single monster attack did any damage.

She could soak the overpowered strikes from above, so the monsters' comparatively dinky bolts were hardly going to do anything.

"Thunderbolt Alley!"

Velvet's skill only increased the electricity in the air. And the monsters weren't about to ignore a player's attack.

"Go on, dodge that!"

She was hitting lightning monsters with lightning, so it was definitely dealing less than max damage, but her raw output was so high, she was brute-forcing her way through their HP bars.

Like her team-ups with Mii, any partner with high DPS created a powerful combo with Maple's impenetrable defense.

The attacks from monsters and the terrain were both formidable, but if they did no damage, then they were no problem.

"Get 'em, Velvet!"

"You know I will!"

Their damage was slowly adding up. As long as they kept this up, victory was as good as theirs. Maple didn't need to help; she just watched Velvet work.

Continuing to spray lightning, they roamed the area and cleaned out the monsters. Once they hit the quest target, it was time to say good-bye to the lightning zone.

"Even with the rocks acting as lightning rods, it's damn loud."

"Yeah, my ears hurt."

Sometimes the bolts from above had drowned out the noise of the monster attacks. Since the flashes dazzled their eyes, this *should* have been a really tough fight.

With the constant thunder and lightning, they could barely hold down a conversation there—not even in the safe zones or under the protection of Martyr's Devotion.

Once they moved into the next rocky area, the thunder faded into the distance. They took a rest on a random boulder.

"Not many monsters here."

"And no lightning! We can finally relax."

Monsters didn't climb up onto the boulders, so if they sat still, they wouldn't have to fight.

"Thanks a million!" Velvet said. "Having you tank is great!"

"It's kinda my thing!"

"There ain't nobody who can beat you at it. I bet you'll get even more tongues wagging soon!"

It only took one fight against Maple to instantly know how strong she was. That sort of strength never went unnoticed. And Maple was already widely known—if anyone managed to top her, that alone would have been cause for buzz.

If they'd gotten so far in the game without a match for her, it was safe to say none existed.

"Your defense was, like, crazy from event one. Which only makes the mystery deepen..."

"Yeah... You weren't around for that, right?"

"Nope! I joined right after it ended."

"Same as Sally! Did you play a lot of games before?"

"Not as many as Hinata. She roped me into this."

Velvet was being light on the details, but it sounded like she and Hinata knew each other in real life.

"Just like Sally got me to play! Same thing. Not that I've adjusted as well as you."

"I've got a lot to learn!"

"Oh? Really?"

Velvet's moves seemed polished; in hand-to-hand, she was on par with Sally. The way she handled herself in a fight convinced Maple that she had lots of experience.

"So Hinata wanted to game with you?"

"Yeah, but she had a different motivation this time."

"Huh?"

"......Practice. Starting with the look."

"...?"

Maple looked baffled, so Velvet cleared her throat and straightened.

"......Well? Do I look genteel and refined now?"

Velvet clasped her hands together, smiling softly. Her usual energy faded, replaced by a reserved disposition. Not at all like an infighter who'd punch you with lightning.

"Wow! You're like a totally different person!"

"Whew. It don't come naturally! Wears me out."

"I like you as you normally are, too!"

"Yeah? Sweet! But fact is, I gotta get good at it. I'm supposed to be one of them proper ladies in real life."

"Huh? Seriously?"

That would explain why her whole vibe changed so dramatically—more than you'd expect for a simple role-play. Maybe one came more naturally to her than the other, but clearly both modes had a lot of time put into them.

"It's true! So Hinata suggested this might be a good place to rehearse."

No one around knew the real Velvet. Even if she switched back and forth, it was a game and wouldn't have any real-life repercussions. The perfect place to perfect the act.

Still, it was hard to change your core personality. Maple hadn't known her long, but she could tell it hadn't fully paid off.

They talked a while longer.

"You play anything else, Maple?"

"Not at all. Never stuck with anything this long!"

"And you went straight to guild master? You were just born like this, then?"

"I wouldn't say that! Sally does all the guild's planning, and everyone else has thoughts of their own."

"Everyone pitching in, then? Rad! Hmm…so you're all gonna be on the same side, then?"

"Uh…well, I talked to Mii and Pain, but we're still thinking."

"So you ain't picked a camp?"

"Not yet."

"Well, I'm going the opposite of where you go!"

She'd promised as much on the eighth stratum, and she would be a fearsome opponent.

"Hnggg…then maybe we'd better keep it secret till the last second and trick you into being on our side…"

Thunder Storm was a powerful guild. Only upsides to teaming with them.

"Good plan! Sally's idea?"

"She hasn't said anything specific, but knowing Sally, she's got all sorts of schemes."

Maple had started to learn a thing or two herself. She might not be able to copy how Sally moved, but she could guess how her friend thought.

"Your guild going with you, Velvet?"

"We're letting everyone pick for themselves! But me and Hinata are stuck together!"

Just as Velvet wanted to fight against Maple, there were players in her own guild who were hoping to fight Velvet herself.

And she welcomed the attempt.

"Big guilds get all sorts of people, huh?"

"Yup! But don't act like this don't concern you, Maple."

"Right…"

Maple had her own guild. Not many members, so a different scale, but they did need to make sure they were all on the same page for this event.

"Can't wait for it to start!"

"Be on our siiide!"

"Never!"

Miming psychic messages at each other, each knew the final decision was a ways off.

◆□◆□◆□◆□◆

After exploring the ninth stratum for a while, Maple Tree were starting to get the hang of which places had strong foes and which didn't.

Armed with loads of intel, they met up in their Guild Home to report in.

To facilitate that, they spread out a large map of the stratum on the table and stood around it, writing in what they'd learned.

"Wow, we've found out so much!"

Sally's monster guide was so uber-complete she couldn't even fit it all, so this map was only terrain, hiding spots, and notes on area status effects. But that alone was far more detailed than the original map.

"I've got another sheet with my materials on it, and Sally's got a third with her monsters."

"Give mine a look over when you've got time. There's a lot more on there than you'll see online, plus notes on how to handle them geared specifically toward Maple Tree members."

"That's amazing. Knowing the right approach in advance makes all the difference."

"Yeah, I'll have a look, pound it into my brain. Best if we have someone other than Sally who can share that info on short notice."

With Kanade's memory, he'd have the whole guide memorized before the day was done. Possibly before this meeting ended.

It was written to be easily skimmed, but you couldn't exactly stop to look things up in combat. Best to learn what they could.

"Course, if Mai and Yui are with you, the approach is pretty much always the same."

"Well, yeah."

Approach, and hammer. The end. The only things that didn't cover were monsters like the lightning balls Maple fought, and in that case, they just had to apply an element first.

Landing a hit meant victory. That even applied to some bosses—the twins played by rules of their own, ignoring all the finer details of combat. It was all too common for them to vaporize bosses before the second phase, when boss monsters added more powerful attack patterns.

"We should all have a look."

"Yeah, *we* can't exactly one-shot your average mob."

If they busted out their biggest guns, maybe, but most times they'd wind up chipping away at each other. They'd need to be cautious around foes with tricky attacks.

As they were discussing things, all the guild members received a message.

"Oh, info on the next event!"

"Um…lots of new details here."

Everyone had known the tenth event was coming, and the broad strokes, but had been forced to speculate on the finer points. At long last, the full rules were here.

They started reading.

"Two camps, one in each kingdom. You'll belong to whichever side you're registered to the day before the event begins. Anyone not on the ninth stratum yet will be able to make their choice, but if they don't make one, they'll be automatically assigned to even out the numbers."

"Makes sense."

"Terrain and monsters will remain as is. Called it! Oh, that's fascinating."

"Monsters on your side won't attack…and there's items in town that'll make them obey limited commands. Kind of like the monsters we tamed?"

They hadn't seen that coming. If it wasn't just players on the defensive lines, that meant more numbers and complications for whoever went on the offensive.

The item effect only lasted five minutes, which wasn't *that* long, but taking advantage of monster skills could provide more strategic options.

And the effect running out merely meant you couldn't give

them detailed orders. They still wouldn't attack your side, which was a boon.

If you got the monsters to the fight, your opponents couldn't exactly ignore them.

"Doesn't seem like you can bring *every* monster, but it's certainly something to look out for."

That wasn't the end of the monster news—since *all* players could join the event, some monster abilities were restricted. There were also areas where players over a certain level would be hit with similar limitations; in other words, player levels determined where they could really shine.

"Best to fight where you're meant to be," Kanade said. "Even I've leveled myself enough to hit these restrictions."

"If you and the twins are affected, basically anyone who's made it to the ninth stratum would be," Sally said.

She was right. All three of them had builds that let them punch above their actual levels, but the average player needed much higher levels to get here at all.

So if these restrictions affected them, these zones were very much meant for low-level players.

In further rules, the monsters were set to launch regular offenses on the enemy camps.

Players could join these waves, attacking with them—that would likely be a core strat.

"It says the town NPCs will help with defense!"

"Ah…they're gonna be key, then. Think they'll use the cannons?"

"Hard to tell how strong they are. They aren't showing any numbers here, so hard to rely on them."

"Good point."

Sally's read said the NPCs would be limited to supporting roles, and that alone would not keep the town safe.

"Three days, and time will be accelerated. Or until one side touches the enemy throne…"

Maple nodded. A successful offense could lead to a swift victory…or an equally swift defeat.

If neither side managed to reach the throne, then the side with the least eliminated players won.

There was a clear need to shore up your defenses to prevent invasion. Otherwise, an individual powerhouse—Maple, Pain, Mii, Velvet, etc.—would just blow right through, bringing a ghastly end to the proceedings.

And the next line in the message put a damper on any such power plays.

"One death and you're out, huh? …Harsh."

"That makes each foe you beat count. A clear loss to the other side."

A single mistake, and you were gone. That would definitely prevent suicide runs. And force everyone to think about how to keep their front line alive in the face of all those incoming hits.

If a loss was one-sided, the number balance would shift—and lead to future losses.

Naturally, there was still the possibility of forcing their way to the throne and scoring a come-from-behind victory. They couldn't let their guard down, even if they were winning.

"Whoa, that's nuts. Look here!" Chrome said.

Maple scrolled farther down, wondering what he meant. Sally got there first and read it aloud.

"'Players and monsters on the same side are treated as party members within a set range.' That what you mean?"

"Yup! With Maple…"

"That means Martyr's Devotion works on everyone."

"Exactly!"

Everyone here knew precisely how strong that was. Skills that normally only worked on party members were now just basic AOEs—functionally, a huge increase to the number of players Maple could protect.

That would make holding a position extremely easy. And it would help that Maple's skill was so well-known. She wouldn't have to explain it; they'd see her in angel form and know what was up.

"Gotta take advantage of it!"

"Yeah, do that…but I guess first, since we're talking about it… we're all gonna be on the *same* side, right?"

"I guess we never really settled that."

"Right… I was just assuming we would be."

"Maple, thoughts?"

"I…was gonna ask everyone to weigh in."

"Fair. Can't plan till we're on the same page."

"Yeah, true. Um…personally, I'd rather fight *with* you all," Maple said.

Everyone nodded. They'd seen that coming, and arguably, that was all Maple Tree needed.

"You're okay with that, Sally?"

"Me? Yeah, if you're in, I'm in."

"Then the members of Maple Tree will all join the same camp!"

Still on the docket: the alliance with the Order, which side to take, and any special prep they needed to get themselves ready.

"Let's get down to it. I can say right off, Mai and Yui are easily taken out but a major threat to the other side. You're gonna be targeted."

"W-we will?"

"Urgh… What do we do?"

"We'll just have to guard you heavily. It won't be just us—our allies will do the same. They've all seen what you did against those raid bosses."

Friends and foes alike knew the twins were at the top of the game.

Not much time left, but that didn't change much. Maple Tree would just have to be as ready as they could be.

With the event specifics announced, players all over changed their approach. The need for intel on monsters and terrain was even greater—more and more players were roaming the fields, and far fewer players were completing quests.

They had only so much time left, and what they needed was all too clear. The quests would still be there after the event, so they simply weren't a priority.

That meant there were far fewer players in town, too. Lots of people put off making a final decision, making sure they'd checked all the areas their guild was lacking intel on.

Maple, however, was still doing the same thing she'd been doing: exploring as she pleased.

Unrelated to any quests, she was back at the castle.

"We're going to be attacking or defending this. I wanna see more of it!"

The quests never took them to the castle; unless players made the conscious choice, they'd only visit that first time. Maple, however, knew the town and the castle interior could turn into battlefields. It would help if she knew what connected to what and where the wide-open spaces, narrow corridors, and dead ends were.

She also just thought it would be fun to tour the castle.

Since the two towns and castles were so similar, she only had to look at one.

Maple was still working the fiery wasteland, so the halls around her were mostly black stone.

"It's huge! Does this count as a dungeon?"

It had certainly been designed with the event in mind—the corridors forked a lot, there were lots of stairs, and it was every bit as easy to get lost in as a proper dungeon. The throne room was at the very back. Unless you wiped out the opposition, players would find themselves chased through the interior, and the defense would know where the offense was headed. They'd need to know the shortest route to avoid getting lapped.

Since the soldiers had already led them on the shortest route to the throne, Maple got one to show her the way again, taking notes. After that, she began exploring.

"What's in here? Hello!"

She found herself in a kitchen, where NPCs in chef hats were cooking.

"I—I shouldn't be here..."

But this was just a game. The cooks kept right on cooking, not reacting to her at all.

As she wondered if there was anything hidden there, her screen popped up.

"Whoa! Um...huh, if I give them ingredients, they'll make food that helps heal or buff us."

Functional locations all came with appropriate explanations—a fact Maple appreciated.

She saw a floating symbol, went over to it, and had them cook something for her. There was a floating screen she could use to place an order.

Maple found something they could make with what she had

on hand and selected that. They handed it over, and she left the kitchen.

"Let's take a look."

She took the food out of her inventory: a well-roasted chunk of meat on the bone.

"Whoa! It's huge!"

It raised all stats, but with Maple's build, that only worked on VIT. A simple snack made from basic monster meat.

Certainly a very "roughing it" meal. Maple put it back in her inventory to eat later and resumed her exploration.

"I bet the king here eats meat like that a lot! She is a dragon…"

On the lookout for anything else interesting, she wandered the castle halls—and found quite a bit. There were bedrooms, workshops like the one Iz had, storehouses for cannon shells, weapons, and food.

And one thing that directly related to the recent admin news.

"Oh! That's it! The Mana Mass! I wonder what it's made of?"

She'd come across a blobby blue ball. Examining the flavor text, she learned this was what would allow players to order some monsters around during the event.

"Looks like you can only carry ten, so you'll have to resupply!"

Sally had said these were also found in warehouses around town. Resupplying there would probably be faster than visiting the castle.

What she'd learned was that you could acquire supplies in the field, town, and castle; if their lines got pushed back, limiting their movements, they could still get the minimum supplies they needed.

If they found themselves under siege, then players like Iz and Marx—assuming they'd survived—would really help their side's planning. Maybe even thwart all incomers until the sides were evened out again. Laying ambushes could be very powerful.

Fill your inventory up ahead of time, and three days wasn't *that* long. You wouldn't even run out of items.

Still, Maple hadn't thought things through that far; she would simply explain what she'd seen to the rest of her guild.

Sally and the more experienced players would make sense of whatever intel she brought back.

"What else is there?"

Maple opened another big door, peering in, and found rows of shelves stuffed full of books. There were stairs nearby, leading to the second floor.

"Whoa! I bet Kanade will wind up reading all of them."

If these books were readable, it would take Maple years to get through them.

But this was a huge library. Two stories of shelves, each so tall Maple couldn't even reach the top shelf.

Maple would usually turn right around and leave, but since Kanade tried teaching her that new language on the last stratum and urged her to look around libraries more the next chance she got, she decided to at least go all the way to the back.

"Maybe there are some interesting books!"

Moving through the center corridor, she found side passages leading in either direction, each lined with shelves. Glancing back and forth, she went all the way back. From what she saw, every book was thick and looked very highbrow.

"Even one of these would take ages!"

Without anything clearly popping out at her, they all looked the same...but as she walked, she passed through something sticky.

"...?"

Assuming she'd walked into something, she rubbed her face... but came up empty. She looked back but saw the same shelves she'd walked past.

"Is my mind playing tricks on me?"

The sensation had been too pronounced for that, so Maple didn't look convinced, but she couldn't find anything that seemed to explain it.

"Welp, gonna see what's back there, then leave! Huh?"

She'd turned toward the back of the room again, and near the back wall, she found a staircase leading down.

No fancy embellishments, just a pit in the floor—and thus, invisible from a distance.

"Three stories?! Wow, this place *is* huge. Kanade has got to check it out!"

After deciding to check out the second floor later, Maple went down the stairs.

The stairs were made of stone, and there were no lights on the walls. This was a departure from the library above.

"Better not take a tumble here… Uh… I need a light…"

Maple took out a light Iz had made for her and turned it on. It was ball-shaped and would hover nearby once activated, lighting up the area. Very useful. And unlike lanterns, it left her hands free.

Rough-hewn walls, the same stone as the stairs themselves. Any player would assume this was a dungeon entrance.

But it was inside the castle, and there were no monsters. Just Maple's footsteps echoing in the darkness.

She went on for a while, and at last, her light revealed a door ahead.

"Is that it?"

She glanced around before opening the door, but the area was as featureless as the stairs. Figuring she'd just have to go in, she grabbed the knob. With a push…the door swung open.

Maple stepped inside. No one had been here in a while—the

wind from the open door was kicking up dust, caught in the glow of her light.

"Do they no longer use this place?"

Like the floor above, this had clearly been a library. There were shelves on both sides and a number of books left behind on them.

Maple headed farther in, taking a good look around before she headed back.

"You never know...um, but all I see is weird books."

Most shelves were empty. Those that weren't didn't have much on them. The remaining books had fallen over, and she could see the covers without pulling them off the shelf—but the covers were all fitted with creepy eyes that looked almost real, gave the impression they were pulsing, or had dark red splatters on the covers. Not exactly well looked after, and not exactly the sort of visuals that made Maple want to look inside.

"The books upstairs were much nicer looking. I'd rather read one of those."

Most didn't even have titles; with no way of knowing what they even were, she had no reason to investigate further.

She settled for making a loop of the room, as planned. As she was about to turn back, she heard a sound *other* than her footsteps.

Behind her. Right at her ear.

"......Come here."

"Yikes?! Wh-who was that?!"

A raspy male voice made Maple spin around...where she found nothing but darkness. She'd been sure someone was standing right behind her, but if that had been true, they'd vanished from view faster than even Sally could move.

Maple hadn't recognized the voice, so it wasn't a friend playing a prank. She looked around again but didn't see anything that looked like the source.

She didn't think she'd imagined it, though. She decided to take a better look at the shelves.

"Over here."

"Ah! Again!"

She'd certainly been startled, but the voice wasn't doing any harm. For lack of better clues, she followed the voice's directions, getting closer and closer.

It led her to a stand—not a shelf—about chest height. There was a book on the stand, wrapped in a strip of cloth covered in red letters and sealed, so no one could read it.

"Just open it."

"You sure? ………Argh, it's gone now!"

Since the voice wasn't answering, she went ahead and did what it had said.

"Do I unwrap this?"

She picked up the book and peeled off the cloth. A strong wind blew from it, and a red glow—like from a magic circle—filled the room.

The gust had blown Maple back, and she quickly realized this was bad. She crawled back to the stand, closed the book, and wrapped it up again.

That must have been the right choice, because the wind died down, and the library was silent again.

"What a shocker! Wonder what that was?"

"A big help. I'll need to borrow your magic a spell."

"Whoooa… Who *are* you?!"

Once more, she searched for the voice—but there was no one there but Maple.

While she was unsure what to do about this disembodied voice…a door slammed open behind her.

"Yikes! Th-the king?!"

The dragonewt monarch she'd met earlier in the throne room. She advanced on Maple and examined her face.

"How'd you get in here?"

"Um…down the stairs?"

"He must have deemed you a comrade and invited you in. Hmm…"

She grabbed Maple's cheeks and tugged.

"Hng! Huat har hou hoing?!"

"If a grimoire likes you…are you really human? If I tear off your skin, what horrors lie beneath?"

The king let go, and Maple backed away.

"Nothing!" she yelped.

She had enough weirdness going on these days that something might well pop out, and she was arguably closer to "horrors" than most monsters the game offered. But she was still firmly in the human category.

"Suit yourself, but coexisting with that will consume you. Consider it your punishment for trespassing."

With that, the king placed her hands together and backed slowly away. Dark red sparks flew, and a mirror appeared, large enough for Maple to see her entire body.

Figuring she was meant to look, Maple moved to it—and could not believe her eyes.

"Wh-what the…?!"

"Better do something before the thing inside you turns you into a desiccated corpse!"

Black stripes ran up Maple's neck, covering half her face, like face paint. She rubbed at it, but it wasn't coming off. It looked a lot like it was corrupting her body.

As Maple's lips flapped wordlessly, a quest was forced upon her.

"Taboo Master… Urgh, never heard of this…"

Neither Sally nor Mii had mentioned this quest, so she had no clue what to do.

"You won't be able to use magic like that! Perish, and I'll gather your bones. Don't want this getting anyone else."

"Uhhh…?"

Maple checked her skills and found they were all unavailable—even ones on her equipment. Her patented defense was largely derived from passives and was fine, but now she was *just* super durable.

The king made it sound like she'd have to finish the quest to resolve things, but the event was almost on them.

"I've gotta hurry!"

Maple ran out of the castle.

----

835 Name: Anonymous Greatsworder
Crisis! Your girl's gone wild!

836 Name: Anonymous Archer
It's a fashion statement.

837 Name: Anonymous Spear Master
Who?

838 Name: Anonymous Greatsworder
Maple!

839 Name: Anonymous Spear Master
Oh…

840 Name: Anonymous Mage
Wild, shmild. I seen her, but she ain't changed inside.

841 Name: Anonymous Greatsworder
I passed her on the street, but half her face was covered in these black marks!

842 Name: Anonymous Spear Master
Side effect from some skill?
I can think of plenty that might do that...

843 Name: Anonymous Archer
And it could be a cosmetic thing!

844 Name: Anonymous Mage
Her sensibilities aren't exactly normal, but it don't feel like her style.

845 Name: Anonymous Great Shielder
Whassup.

846 Name: Anonymous Greatsworder
You're her guardian!
You're supposed to keep her from going bad!

847 Name: Anonymous Great Shielder
We talked it over.
Figured she grows more when she's doing her own thing.

848 Name: Anonymous Archer
Time to change your educational approach!
Please!!

849 Name: Anonymous Spear Master
She's become even less human...
And we blame you.

850 Name: Anonymous Great Shielder
Ain't it grand?

851 Name: Anonymous Mage
Are you a mad scientist?

852 Name: Anonymous Great Shielder
I ain't heard a peep about this yet, so it *could* be cosmetic.

853 Name: Anonymous Spear Master
It's not completely impossible.
The stores do sell face paint.

854 Name: Anonymous Great Shielder
But what you're saying seems unlikely.
If she went for that, it would be like...cute?

855 Name: Anonymous Spear Master
There you have it.
Ugh, pour one out for her humanity.
We blame you!

856 Name: Anonymous Greatsworder
Don't let the cuties leave home!

857 Name: Anonymous Archer
I've never heard of a skill that permanently alters your appearance, so it might not be one.

858 Name: Anonymous Great Shielder
The event's coming up fast, better run at her and see what it does.

859 Name: Anonymous Greatsworder
At least look for yourself!

860 Name: Anonymous Mage
The stripes are *black.* That's never good...

861 Name: Anonymous Spear Master
Letting her play her way makes her stronger...low investment...

862 Name: Anonymous Archer
But skills compatible with Maple are few and far between, so even if it's a good one, it may not be much use.

863 Name: Anonymous Mage
Stat buffs are pointless for her.

864 Name: Anonymous Greatsworder
I say that ALL the time!
But it's *never* paid off.

865 Name: Anonymous Mage
Please! Let us off the hook this once!

866 Name: Anonymous Archer
People! We have but one option! Join the same side she does!

If she was an ally, they had nothing to fear. And in the event, her buffs would help even more people—if this was another one of those skills, the more the merrier.

The members of this forum made sure to report this news to their respective guilds.

CHAPTER 5

Defense Build and Full Company

While others feared for her future, Maple herself was quite worked up herself and promptly ran straight to Iz.

A quest had been forced upon her; some mystery thing was sealed within her body, and the price for that was far too steep.

Her MP was being absorbed, never recovering and always staying at zero. Any skills that required her to say the name out loud—even if they were on her gear—were currently locked.

This meant she could not even use the Awaken skill to call out her pet monster.

Maple's remaining offensive repertoire was basically *only* Devour, a skill that activated automatically. Fundamentally, the game didn't have many attack skills that *didn't* require you to yell the name.

"Iz!" she cried, bursting into the Guild Home.

Iz was nearly always in her workshop, and sensing something amiss, she came running out.

"What's wrong? Oh dear. Your face..."

Half of Maple's face was covered in black markings. Something clearly was not right. Not blind to that, Iz moved on to what she could do.

"If you're coming to me, is this some item? I can cure most status effects."

Iz could make things faster than they got used in combat or sold to other players, so her inventory was always stacked high with consumables.

"I've got plenty of those… Uh, look!"

Maple showed Iz the progress screen for the quest she was on.

"Sacrifice equipment…? Never seen a requirement like that. Not your standard fetch quest."

"There's lots of different brackets, and I think I drop stuff in them!"

Maple opened her inventory and pointed out a few spots. There were black brackets at the bottom of her inventory, and the quest text suggested dropping things in them would progress the quest.

"Then lemme give you something. I've got plenty that aren't in use."

Iz's inventory *also* had a whole pile of spare equipment she'd made. Pieces where the design hadn't lived up to her ideals, older works where the specs weren't up to what the current stratum demanded and would never see the light of day, and things she'd bought at other shops for reference. Plenty of stuff she could just give Maple.

Maple took one of the items from her, put it in the designated bracket, and checked the display to see if it got absorbed.

"Please work…!"

"Looks like it did."

Maple double-checked; what Iz had given her was nowhere to be found, but the quest progress had advanced incrementally.

"Okay, that's the right approach…but that's only, like, one percent!"

There was a yellow bar right below the quest name, providing a visual reference for progress, but the change was so slight it might be mistaken for a trick of the eyes.

"Wonder if better gear moves it further?"

Iz took another piece out of her inventory and had Maple try that.

Her prediction seemed accurate; progress might improve with better-quality gear, equipment with skills on it, or items enhanced with her Smithing skill.

"Well, it did say 'absorb.' Naturally, it would want to absorb better things."

Iz was rifling through her inventory for the next piece.

"Are…you sure? They're gone for good!"

"It's fine. This is all stuff that wasn't getting used anyway, and you'd struggle with this on your own, right?"

Lord knew how much equipment she'd have to purchase to get through this solo.

Iz's assistance was a huge relief.

"It's sealed all my skills, and I've got no MP! I can't exactly ransack dungeons for gear. With my defense, I'd *survive*, but…"

"Really? Well, we'd better fix this quick, then. I was planning on seeing it through either way, mind."

"You were?"

"Of course. I mean, I bet this gives you a new skill—right before the big event. If you get stronger, that helps all of us."

"Oh!"

Whatever potential skill Maple might acquire was likely more valuable than a hundred things taking up space in Iz's inventory. Rather than let that collect dust, it was better to get their ultimate weapon a whole new skill.

"Go right ahead and take what you need!"

"Thanks so much!"

For a while, Maple absorbed the contents of Iz's inventory.

"But what is it we think it's absorbing?" Iz asked.

"It's like there's a weird guy inside me? I think he's eating them!"

"Th-that sounds alarming..."

If Maple's phrasing was accurate, he was even less discriminate than Maple (who regularly ate monsters).

"So it seals off your skills. Any other problems?"

"I'm fine otherwise!"

In hindsight, having some mystery thing inside you was pretty alarming, but it seemed to bother Maple far less than Iz thought.

"Then good. Let's just keep feeding it until this quest is done!"

"Great!"

If they could wrap this up, no use waiting around; best to power through. Whatever she got for completing it would affect the event. If it *was* a skill, Maple would need time to practice with it, so the sooner they finished, the better.

Both had time right now, so Iz was planning on seeing it through.

Iz wasn't kidding about her stock—her inventory was full of gear far better than anything found in shops but which she'd never found a buyer for.

Whatever was hiding inside Maple was every bit as voracious as Maple herself, and it swallowed well over a hundred pieces of equipment. Still, there *was* an end to it eventually; the bar was nearly at 100 percent.

"It really requires a *lot*. Astounding."

"Sorry...!"

"You're always bringing me tons of materials, so don't sweat it. You scratch my back, I scratch yours."

The last bit of gear was absorbed, and the quest was marked complete—and immediately replaced with a new quest.

"Augh!"

"More to it, then."

They checked what came next, and it required Maple to slay a bunch of monsters solo. A rather tall order in her current state.

"If you've gotta be solo, we can't even help..."

The first quest was *meant* to be time-consuming, but Iz had managed to completely negate that. Most players would likely find this next phase easier, but not Maple.

Maple's build fundamentally didn't let her do much damage just waving a weapon around.

She might get by on the first stratum, where the enemies had no defense, but with the higher minimum stats on the ninth stratum, she could easily stab a monster a hundred times with her short sword and not even do a single point of damage.

"I can't use Syrup, either...or Atrocity..."

"The fact that you *could* attack was hardly normal, but this is an impasse."

She'd had skills sealed before, but never all of them at once. Iz had heard about mages struggling in areas that sealed their spells, but skills were even worse.

"Welp, I guess I'll give you a bunch of items. They'll help! They're how I fight."

Iz began taking out handmade bombs and other attack items.

Every one of them was so powerful it would make you think Iz was a damage-dealing class.

These would allow Maple to slay monsters despite her attack stat. Naturally, Iz had lots of skills that buffed item effects, so they wouldn't be as powerful in Maple's hands, but her patented defense gave her far more time to stand around throwing items, which largely solved that problem.

"Heh-heh, I hope this skill's a good one! But let's not assume this quest is the last one."

"Right! But I do wanna wrap it up before the event."

"That's the spirit!"

Iz promised to craft any items she ran low on and saw Maple out.

Outside town, Maple was wandering the field. Unable to ride Syrup or to use Atrocity, traveling anywhere took forever. She was headed for a flat area with frequent spawns and lots of monsters, a popular destination for players looking to grind levels.

According to Sally's guide, nothing here was especially strong; lots of animal types, so plenty of them were quick on their feet, but none had piercing skills.

No armor piercing—that was Maple's sole condition. Without access to Pierce Guard, and no skills to fight back with, she couldn't exactly fight a foe her defense wouldn't work on.

Naturally, there were other players here grinding, so spotting her walking around drew some reactions—"Weird, she's actually on foot!" "She's in her human form!"—but they soon spotted those marks and looked suitably alarmed.

"She's got something on her face!"

"Her eyes and hair change colors all the time, but…that sure looks like a curse."

This was clearly not a good thing, and the other players watched with bated breath, imagining all manner of terrifying outcomes. But instead, Maple just found a relatively empty corner and opened her inventory.

"This, and this…"

She took out a little bottle of pink fluid, popped the lid, and scattered it around.

Nearby monsters all aggroed on her, charging in.

"Wow! That's really effective!"

This was one of Iz's creations, a monster lure. The eighth event had proved that making enemies come to her was faster than chasing after them. There were lots of big monsters here—bears and wolves, etc.—so once they pounced on her, she got knocked on her back. But like the guide said, no piercing attacks, and no damage done.

"Now this!"

Maple had taken out two items before the fight. The second was a large pot. With all these monsters on her, it soon cracked, which was the goal.

When it cracked, the liquid within sprayed everywhere.

It was a viscous fluid that enhanced the effects of other items— oil, basically.

Now prepped, she put a crystal in each hand and crushed them.

Flames spewed from her left hand; lightning from her right. The sparks ignited the oil, while the lightning spread across the zone like a spider's web.

All monsters lured in kept attacking despite this damage, but Maple just lay there, waiting for items to do their work.

Players watching merely saw fire and electricity. They couldn't tell she'd used items.

"What's she doing now?!"

"Brutal..."

"This is as bad as the poison..."

No one had an accurate understanding of her current situation, so they just assumed the marks on her face were related to the attacks they saw—and concluded it was a new skill.

Everyone knew Maple was forever finding crazy skills, and one side of this stratum was all about these two elements. With everyone eager to learn about other players' builds, this was a logical conclusion.

"Not all that high damage, though…?"

"Maybe there's side effects?"

It was actually just regular items, a strategy Maple was forced to resort to. But it gave everyone the impression she had a powerful counter she could use on anything that got too close— and inadvertently helped keep her safe from pierce attacks in the future.

Maple spent a while sprawled out on the ground, incinerating incoming monsters with her items. A fire perpetually burning in one corner of the field, impossible to see through. Quite a few players heard this was Maple, made observations, and took that intel home.

Blissfully unaware of this, Maple just waited for the quest to end.

"Hnggg, this is all I *can* do!"

Occasionally, she used a bomb, too, gradually adding to the number slain. Items were her sole means of attack, and she had few options for increasing damage; she was forced to simply wait it out. But the items Iz made did a lot to reduce the time this would have taken Maple otherwise.

"Just a bit more for today!"

Like she'd told Iz, she wanted this quest done before the event— and had no clue how many more stages there were. It did not hurt to power through this one.

While Maple was out soloing hordes, Chrome and Kasumi returned to the guild.

"Yo, Iz. Not crafting today?"

"Chrome! I was just helping Maple out."

"Yeah? I heard the rumors. Some sort of face paint thing?"

"Oh, it's getting around already? That's what she was asking me about."

"What's going on?" Kasumi asked. "This is news to me."

"She's got a multi-stage quest that left her like that. Not sure if it leads to a skill or equipment, but…"

"Ah! I thought so. Just as we'd hoped!"

"I dunno if I'd say that…but she really does stumble into stuff."

"This one's pretty rough, though. She said there's something inside her, and it's preventing her from using any skills but her passives."

"Yeesh. Like a curse? That is bad."

"With Maple's stats, she's virtually helpless. The more skill-dependent your build, the worse that restriction is."

"I helped her get through the first stage."

"Oh? It wasn't combat, then?"

"No. It was a lot like crafting quests where you turn in the stuff you make. The thing inside her consumed over a hundred pieces of equipment. And the strength of what you fed it seemed to matter— quite the gourmand."

"That's…a lot. But does suggest the final reward will be a doozy."

"Yeah. Iz had that stuff on hand, so it might not feel like it, but that's a lot of resources. And she's off to the next step?"

"Now she's gotta solo slay a bunch of monsters. I gave her a heap of attack items. Only way she can fight right now."

"Hard to help if she's gotta play solo… I guess we could farm the materials for these items?"

"That would help me, yes. It seemed like she'd need a *lot*. And with the event coming up, I don't want to be short-stocked."

"Then I'll pitch in. Let Maple know we're available with any-thing she needs."

"Good. I appreciate it!"

"Cool! If we get Maple one more power-up, we're set."

"We've done enough work on the map. Completing Maple's quest is now our top priority."

"I'll tell the others what's up. They've each got different strengths. She should ask the right peeps for the job."

If they were aware of the issue ahead of time, that made it eas-ier to get going. While Maple was forced to play solo, they would get everyone up to speed.

They'd told Maple to play like this, and it was finally paying off. Well worth the time it would take them to back her up.

"I'll head out right now."

"Lemme come with. Riding Haku speeds things up."

"Good luck! I don't mind what you bring; just bring what you can. I can always convert it to cash if I've got enough."

"You've got a skill for that, right? Okay, we'll grind some out."

"Thanks!"

Chrome and Kasumi headed out to the field to support Iz—and by extension, Maple.

Maple spent the next few days logging in and generating a pillar of fire on the plains. At long last, she was almost at the quest target.

Iz kept her stocked up on items, and occasionally Kasumi, Sally, or the twins helped her get there and back. It was a long haul slaying monsters with items alone, slowly but steadily grinding through the quest.

"Okay! Last one!"

The bomb she'd used killed a monster—and the quest was completed.

"Whew…that took forever!"

For a player who didn't usually use items to suddenly make them her primary weapon, that was a tall order. The fact that she'd pulled it off at all was entirely down to her defense nullifying all their attacks, which allowed her to keep fighting until her item supply ran out.

"Is that the end of it?"

Maple checked her quest log, but sadly, there was more to it.

"Hmm…uh, item gathering?"

All sorts of items were listed; some far harder to get than others. Common materials like monster meat—available even on the first stratum—to super-rare stuff like dragon wings, which only dropped from tough foes. Even stuff like demon hearts that she didn't even know where to get.

"Guess I'll ask the others!"

Maple Tree's members had fought all manner of monsters. Rare items often proved memorable, and they might know how to get them.

Maple fired off a message to the other members and headed back to the Guild Home.

She was far out of town and could only move on foot, so by the time she got back, the others were all assembled.

"Sorry! I'm the last one!"

"You're on the next leg of this quest?"

"Yup! I gotta find all kinds of items!"

"Really? Got a list?"

"Can we share this?"

Sally looked at Maple's quest, then put it on the big screen so everyone could see.

"Interesting. I've seen most of these. I bet you've got some yourself."

"Everyone check your inventories, and let's mark what we already have."

"Yeah. Um…I might not be much use here. Do I *have* anything rare?"

"Mai and me have the same stuff!"

"Mm-hmm, you *are* always together."

Everyone went through their inventories, comparing them against the list.

The eight of them had scoured most of the ninth floor. Almost all the items were found in someone's inventory.

"But not this demon heart."

"Yeah. Guess we'll have to track down relevant monsters."

"Oh!" Maple said. "I've got one! But since when?"

"Maybe the one you got Atrocity from? Or the mock Maples in the eighth event?"

"Could be!"

"There you have it…"

"I bet Maple's got the weirdest item collection. All I've got is standard field drops."

"We're doing pretty well here…"

"Um, yeah, only a few left to find!"

It was less a question of finding them than gathering the right number. Everything they were short on, they knew where to get.

And the reasons for the shortage were clear—these monsters usually had low drop rates or didn't give much XP, so nobody had spent time fighting them.

"Then let's split up and bang this out! Doesn't say Maple has to do this one all her own."

"Thanks a lot!"

When they could all pitch in, that made things way faster. Monsters with low drop rates would require a lot of kills and were not a great choice for Maple in her condition.

With their plans drawn up, they all headed out to tackle monsters right for their builds.

◆□◆□◆□◆□◆

Maple Tree had split into multiple teams to gather the quest materials. The first of these was Sally, Kasumi, and Maple.

Unable to rely on Martyr's Devotion, she was unable to back up the twins the way she usually did, and she needed someone else doing damage. That made this current team the obvious choice.

They could, of course, fight solo—but having Maple with them meant they could exploit their AGI and duck behind her when a foe used a strong attack. Even in this state, she was nice to have. And they helped provide the mobility options Maple herself had lost.

Currently, Kasumi had Haku use Supergiant, and they were riding the snake across the map.

"Maple, like we said, just try to stay in range."

"You're our get-out-of-dodge plan."

"Mm-hmm!"

She couldn't use Taunt to pull enemies to her, and it wasn't practical to hit things with her sole remaining offensive option, Devour.

That meant her role was to act like an indestructible boulder traipsing around the field, providing cover wherever they went.

If monsters tried to get to the girls hiding behind her, then Devour was an option.

Their snake ride took them to a yawning cavern entrance on the side of a mountain. Not particularly hidden; more of a proper dungeon.

"This the place, Sally?"

"Yup."

"Okay. Haku!"

Kasumi put them down and set her snake back to its default size. It was too big to fit in the cave otherwise.

"I doubt Haku will be much use outside the boss fight."

Her pet's strengths largely assumed Supergiant was active; Haku couldn't do much while small. Not really a monster designed for close-quarters combat.

"But we're not gonna struggle with anything on the way—as long as it can enlarge in the boss room, I don't see the problem."

"Fair. Let's roll with that."

"This cave has rare monsters?"

"Nothing you haven't seen before. A nest of buffed goblins, basically. You…know what those are, right?"

"Yeah! But they're buffed?"

"Yeah, this dungeon has attack and speed buffs applied to all monsters within."

"Huh… Doesn't matter where?"

"Right. Since the buff itself is strong, the spawn rate is rather low."

Their offense was buffed, but not their defense; and goblins weren't exactly spongey to begin with. That meant the fights would go quickly.

"Better save Devour for the boss. We'll handle things on the way."

That's why they'd tagged along. Maple took Kasumi's advice and switched to her white shield. Keeping her Devour shield in her inventory avoided accidental uses.

"Onward!"

"Formation?"

"Let's go with Maple in front, just in case. These monsters *do* have high DPS."

"On it!"

She might not have her skills, but with Maple in the lead, they could avoid an unfortunate strike at the start of a fight. And at Maple's walking speed, she couldn't keep up with the others. Best to have her set the pace.

Thus, they plunged into the dungeon depths. Not long after, they heard noises up ahead.

"……Drums?"

"Sounds like."

A rhythmical, powerful thumping—less like Japanese drums and more like bongos.

"The music grants the buff. Gets stronger the closer we get to the boss room."

"I see. So this'll get steadily harder."

Knowing it was strongest in the boss room meant they had time to adjust to the strength and made it easier to tell when to retreat. A well-designed dungeon.

"Much easier than some of those hidden dungeons we've stumbled across. At the very least, we won't be suddenly trapped in here."

"Yup, yup! It's always nasty when they don't let you run home."

Maple had been yanked into several such dungeons, or

voluntarily leaped into them, so she was aware of how rough they could be.

"It's not supposed to be that common..."

As they talked, they moved forward, emerging in a larger room. Ahead were several giant goblins wielding bloodstained blades, smaller goblins with crossbows, and at the back of the pack, a single goblin with a crown, barking orders.

They seemed to be reinforcing the dungeon walls, working on a wooden barricade in response to the leader's commands.

The passage the girls were in was outside their aggro range, so the goblins weren't charging at them—but the only way forward lay through this room, so a fight was inevitable.

"What you think, Sally?"

"The intel we've got suggests they don't really have any unusual attacks. The crossbows have a mystic power that lets them keep firing without reloading, so those bolts'll be like rain. Anyone not Maple should take care. The sword's what it looks like: high damage, sweep attacks. The leader can bark orders that up their movement speed and attack damage even higher. Also, if you get near the walls on either side, spears'll shoot out."

"Yikes."

"All right. Knowing that ahead of time makes all the difference."

"I figured we might wanna duck into dungeons during the event. I mean, if Maple's with us, we can hide out anywhere, and the monsters'll protect us from invaders."

"I'll stay clear of the walls!"

"Do that. Also, advance warning's different from actually keeping up with their speed. Expect them to be way faster than you'd think a goblin would be."

"I'll bear that in mind."

Knowing your enemy was a powerful asset. If nothing that happened was unexpected, the odds of losing were that much lower.

"Armored Arms!"

Kasumi activated her skill, and she was ready. They stepped into the room. The goblins saw them coming and braced for combat.

"Here goes!"

"Yeah!"

Going for the first strike, Sally took aim at a goblin armed with a crossbow, and Kasumi went after one with a sword.

The smaller goblins turned their weapons toward Sally. Effects shone around the crossbows as they shot two bolts in rapid succession, rocketing her way.

"Hmph!"

Reading their flight paths, she twisted herself, using her dual daggers to slap other bolts aside.

Sally didn't even break stride. She was about to carve into one goblin when the lead barked an order, and red light wreathed all goblins present.

This gave them all a burst of speed. They moved as fast as Sally, backstepping so she couldn't quite get to them.

"Leap!"

Sally used a skill to close the gap, but her daggers just didn't have the reach.

Her slash came up empty. But a moment later, red sparks flew from the goblin's throat.

Her dagger was now a sword—abruptly providing more reach its default shape could not.

There was nothing preventing her from mixing and matching her two unique sets. She was dual wielding, so that alone gave her freedom. Guise let her make them look like whatever she wanted, so no one but Sally herself would ever know which loadout she had equipped. The shapeshifted dagger aside, everything *looked* like her standard blue gear.

The damage made the goblin stagger. Sally closed in, shifting the blade back to a dagger, and piled on a combo.

But this alone was not enough to finish off the goblin. She raised her blades to attack again, but the rest of the goblins aimed their crossbows high.

The bolts they fired split in the air, raining down upon her. The goblin in front of her was pretty beaten up, but it fired a bolt of its own.

With Cover and Martyr's Devotion out of commission, Maple couldn't help. The rain of arrows went right through her.

"Sally!"

"I'm fine!"

Pincushion Sally melted into thin air—and the real Sally appeared behind another goblin.

She quickly stabbed it in the back, then retreated to Maple.

"Argh, that skill always gets me!"

"Ha-ha, sorry."

Her headgear *was* actually the scarf it appeared to be, letting her use Mirage to trick the monsters. It was nigh impossible to tell what Sally was really doing anymore. If you wanted to get the upper hand, you'd have to defeat her in the arena of the mind.

"Gotta try things out if I want to trick real players."

Sally was not using these ruses haphazardly—their true power was only unleashed when they were utterly convincing. Deceit was a highly technical art.

Her new fighting style required far more mental resources than just being dodgy. She figured she at least had to get good at fooling monsters.

*   *   *

Meanwhile, Kasumi was deflecting the giant goblin's great-sword with the blades wielded by her Armored Arms, dancing circles around its bulky frame.

Her Agility might not be as high as Sally's, but it was nothing to sneeze at, and since she had a proper HP pool, her fighting style was far more stable. She could take a few hits and heal back up later—a big difference from Sally's approach.

"Blood Blade!"

Her blade melted, becoming a liquid-y whip that lashed at the goblin's torso from outside the range of its greatsword. It was a tough cookie, and the leader had it buffed. It surged forward, but Kasumi knew her way around a dodge.

And Kasumi had a powerful skill that backed up any such play.

"Mind's Eye!"

This skill displayed red boxes showing where the next attack could land, and while it was active, Kasumi could evade by a hairbreadth—like Sally did.

She slipped past the greatsword's downward swing, her Armored Arms attacking and racking up damage.

"Fifth Blade: Crumble Heart!"

A skill with a powerful stun momentarily stopped her foe in its tracks.

Even with the dungeon effect and the leader's buffs upping their speed, the greatsword goblins were specced heavily into attack. They couldn't keep up with Kasumi.

"Cutting you down!"

She evaded another swing, slashed at it in passing, and turned to the next goblin. It was already swinging, but Mind's Eye had told her that.

"First Blade: Heat Haze!"

A teleport to close in quickly, too close for the swing to connect, and a clean hit.

Kasumi had a bunch of skills that let her make quick moves or teleport around. On her own power, it might be tough to dodge some moves, but the extra burst her skills provided often allowed her to make the necessary adjustments.

If she warped forward after they'd committed to a swing, the blow would have to hit *both* locations to hurt her at all.

"Forth Blade: Whirlwind!"

Her skill attacks hit *hard*, and she was taking out one monster after another.

"Wow! You're both amazing!"

With their leader cheering them on, they carved their way through the goblins.

"And that's all she wrote!"

They'd cleared the minions and felled the goblin leader. Certain there were no reinforcements coming, Sally and Kasumi took a breather.

"Definitely faster than I thought."

"Yeah. And the dungeon buff isn't that strong yet. Gotta keep our wits about us."

"Nice work! Sorry I'm useless right now..."

"That's what happens when your skills are sealed."

"You just relax till we hit the boss. We'll make sure you get there."

If she had all Devour uses left, she could go for a quick finish on the boss. That made the road there even more vital.

"Kasumi, how are you doing on skills?"

"My first time facing them. I used Mind's Eye just in case, but I got a feel for their moves and speed. Should be fine without it."

They knew their enemies would get steadily faster, but she'd been able to track their base speed just fine—and it shouldn't be too hard to adjust to the rest. Foresight and firsthand experience were both vital factors in combat performance.

"There you have it, Maple! Let's move right along."

"Okay! Thanks! Items aren't banned, so I'll use some stuff that buffs your attack!"

"That'll help. Go for it."

Bombs would likely hurt them, too, so she couldn't throw those out, but anything that buffed her allies or debuffed their enemies was risk-free.

They'd made it through the first fight without issue, and that momentum carried them on, deeper into the dungeon.

Maple was basically deadweight—it was a tribute to how strong the other two girls were that they could handle everything without her.

Maple Tree's reputation was often chalked up to the sheer impact of Maple's skill collection, but the rest of the members were all respect-worthy threats.

Minor buffs didn't let monsters with basic attack patterns stand a chance against them.

They just tackled each pack head-on, batted them aside, paid no heed to the increasing buff, and made it safely to the boss room.

The drums were much louder now. The thing affecting the entire dungeon lay behind these doors.

"Maple, Devour...?"

"All good! Didn't use any!"

"There's a ton of goblins inside here, but you know the plan?"

"Yep. Worst comes to worst, I'll do something—if you don't object."

"I do not. This seems like the simplest approach."

The plan was for Maple to stay on her current shield until she was right next to the boss.

Accidentally wasting Devour on the minion goblins would mean she'd kept it in reserve for nothing.

"Opening her up!"

"Ready."

"Good to go."

Confirmations done, they opened the door and stepped inside. A long, wide room, and at the back, a giant beating a drum—the boss. Between them stood a horde of goblins wielding crossbows, greatswords, and spears. Some were even riding lizards, and others were shield-sporting defensive units. All were bristling with fury.

As the drumbeat resounded, a red aura rose from the goblin horde. Their eyes gleamed; they were ready to pounce.

They had the numbers, and each type played their role. A perfect formation. And the buff was at peak stack.

Tensions rose, and both sides leaped into action simultaneously.

"Haku! Supergiant! Harden!"

Her snake's size increased a hundredfold. The goblin's blows bounced off its hardened scales. The first wave blocked, Kasumi got the others on its back and guided Haku to slither across the boss room.

They'd always meant to ignore the adds, going only for the boss itself.

"We know if the big guy goes down, they'll all vanish."

Sally wasn't about to play this to the monster's strengths. If they knew an easier way, she always took it.

"Maple, almost there!" Kasumi called.

"Mm-hmm!"

Maple took out her pitch-black shield. The skill on this could swallow anything it touched. At the moment, it was her sole viable means of attack, but a pretty powerful one.

"Specter of Carnage!"

"Water Cowl! Oboro, Whet Wisp!"

Kasumi and Sally both fired up skills, ready to burst damage this thing.

Haku bit into its shoulder, and the road to the boss was paved. Not one goblin could stop it.

"Quintuple Slash!"

"First Blade: Heat Haze, Third Blade: Blue Moon, First Blade: Heat Haze, Third Blade: Blue Moon!"

Wreathed in fire and water, Sally used a combo move, while Kasumi took full advantage of the cooldown reduction Specter of Carnage provided, chaining skills in midair to drag herself around the boss, Armored Arms adding even more damage.

"Hyah!"

And as the boss focused on them, a tiny figure hopped up on Haku's head, jumping toward the boss's head.

It was more of a body slam than a jump.

Her shield beneath her, Maple let gravity do the work.

This did so much damage she split the boss in half, taking out its head, chest, stomach, and hips as she fell through.

It was over in an instant.

She was on it before it spotted her—and then she'd cut it in half.

That was all.

The two halves exploded into light, and with their boss gone, the remaining goblins scattered to the winds.

"Nice. Made it simple."

"...Forced it to *be* simple."

"That went well!"

"Mm-hmm. Better than I thought. But if you blow ten Devours, that'll do it!"

Ordinarily, she wasn't that cavalier about using it, but they only needed to clear this thing once—no reason to be stingy.

"Okay, Maple. That's the drum we need."

"Oh, right!"

Once it became a drop item, it shrank down to human size. Decorated in patterned vines and jewels, this was their current goal.

A drum called Frenzy. Just like the dungeon effect, if they used this, it would up the party's STR and AGI. But as an item, it had its downsides: It would lower their VIT, INT, and DEX.

"Not the worst. Especially for our guild."

"With Maple in working condition, we don't have to worry about a VIT debuff. Could be useful if we're going on the offense."

"But this one's for Maple's quest. Might wanna come get another later on."

Her quest had demanded this drum—and like Iz's equipment, once she turned it in, the item was lost.

"I'll come with you again!"

"Yeah, and we'll instagib it once more."

"Yep. I don't mind tagging along."

"The plan won't work without you, Kasumi! Please do."

With their objective complete, they left the goblin den.

The other five members of Maple Tree were headed in a different direction. This party was hunting for items Maple needed and had just reached their destination.

Every neck craned upward.

"......That's tall."

"You're...sure it's here?"

"That's what the reports said. Won't know until we get up there."

Before them was a sheer cliff face. More of a towering pillar than a mountain. There were thick stone columns all around, and the tallest of them soared above the clouds.

"There's a bird's nest on top, and you can gather there?"

"Demon Crystals, yup. I think the bird's collecting shiny things?"

They knew they could get it here, but they'd been unable to find any concrete information on the drop rates.

The info came from NPC rumors, and it was unclear if anyone had pulled it off.

"Clearly, no use for anyone but Iz to try."

This was bound to be a very rare drop. Iz had lots of bonuses to rare-drop odds, so she was their best bet. The problem was the climb.

"We use those...platforms?"

"They seem to go around and around, and there's no way in... so I guess so?"

It might go straight up like a column, but the polished surface wasn't entirely free of footholds. There were clearly rocks jutting out for them to climb on.

"I'm not exactly equipped to scale this."

"Me neither."

"Mai and Yui could probably carry us both...but I bet there's more to it."

They could hear sinister birds screeching in the air above. It didn't seem likely they'd let the group climb in peace.

If Mai and Yui died, they'd all go plummeting back to earth. Only Maple could survive that fall.

"Not hearing any better ideas…so let me take this one."

"You got a plan?"

"I do today."

Kanade looked up once again, had them huddle close, and used a skill Akashic Records had just provided.

"Flight."

This skill lifted them all off the ground.

"Whoa!"

"Amazing!"

"This means…"

"Don't get your hopes up. All it does is lift us straight up."

"Huh? Oh, true! I can't move!"

""Ohhh!""

Soon enough, the effect wore off, and they started falling.

"Wood Wall! So…I gotta make platforms to catch us."

A thick branch had emerged from the wall, catching them all.

"Y-you scared me there."

"I figured there was a downside, but…that was a real heart-stopper."

"I made sure there was a proper platform right next to us. Hop to that quick, or you really will fall."

The others scrambled over and scoped out the next foothold.

"Each time Flight gets off cooldown, we'll use that. It doesn't let us move around, but we can use skills—any birds come at us, please take them down."

"Can do!"

"That's our thing!"

"Then I'll stand at the outside edge. Block anything incoming."

"Sounds like a plan!"

They ascended the pillar, getting higher and higher.

"They should spot us soon…see?"

One of the large birds circling overhead wheeled round and swooped toward them. Chrome braced for a dive attack, but it chose to hover, flapping its wings and peppering them with wind blades.

"Yo, what? Multi-Cover!"

They hid behind the great shield, weathering the barrage. Chrome soaked it all, and no wind blades reached the fragile four.

They held out until the winds momentarily died down. The monster was likely taking a break from an advantageous position, but an instant later, something gray pierced its body.

""Here goes!""

Steel balls were thrown by Mai and Yui with their full strength behind them. The resulting impact did just as much damage as Kanade's best spells.

Iz could make a near-infinite supply of ammo for them, so they need not conserve it. They had not just been cowering behind Chrome's shield—they'd been watching for an opening to turn the tables.

Their next throws pierced its wings, crushed its beak, opened more holes in the torso—and the monster exploded.

"Wow, good aim!"

"Impressive. If I tried throwing things at it, I'd never hit."

"We don't have many ranged options!"

"So we practiced a lot!"

This approach was particularly effective against larger monsters. One of their throws need only brush against it to do fatal damage, so it didn't matter where they hit. The bigger the target, the easier that was.

"Keep it up! Easier to slay them at range than to let them get in close."

"If things do go wrong, I've got a grimoire to negate the damage. Take your time and aim."

""Will do!""

Major damage made monsters flinch. If the twins alternated throws, they could prep a new ball while the enemy was flinching and prevent them from moving at all.

"The skill's off cooldown, so let's hover!"

They floated up, moved to a stable platform, and took out the nearby monsters. Rinse and repeat, until they outflew the monster spawns. They passed through the clouds unbothered, and as the ground faded from view, they sighted the top.

"Finally?"

"Looks like."

No monsters were flying about—they safely set foot on the pillar peak.

They'd been less than confident, but the info was right, and there was a giant bird's nest with a single egg inside. The size of this suggested it was even bigger than the bird monsters flying all around, but the nest's occupant was away.

Combat was still in the cards, so Chrome led the way, inching toward the nest. Their fears proved unfounded—and the GATHER icon appeared.

"Okay, Iz! Strut your stuff!"

"On it."

Iz switched her accessories to raise her rare item gather rate, drank a potion, took some pills that looked like supplements, crushed several crystals to the consternation of her audience, and was soon wreathed in multiple auras.

"You…don't look like you're about to *gather*."

"This is essentially where I do battle. Fay, Fairy Luck."

This last skill boosted her rare-drop rate even higher, and at last, Iz stuck her hand in the nest. There was a limit to how many times she could gather, and if they came up empty, they'd have to make the ascent again.

"W-well?"

"Iz, how's it going?"

"I'm so nervous…"

"We'll just have to wait and watch."

"Heh-heh, don't worry. Gathering is my thing! See?"

Iz took something out of her inventory, showing it off: a regular octahedron, black and glistening. Lord only knew what it was made of. It seemed to pulse ominously. And it *was* called a Demon Crystal—the object they'd come looking for.

"Wow! You actually got one?"

"Good news for Maple."

"Nice work, Iz!"

"We really got it in one."

"I splurged and used all those items. They'd better work."

"You dropped them like you would any potion, but I figured they were a big deal…"

"Yes. Raising your rare-drop rate is always a tall order."

"We'll help grind materials for the replacements…"

"Please. But I'm looking at this as an investment."

"Only scary part is—we don't know where it'll lead."

"Personally, I think it's safe to get our hopes up."

The road to a new skill might be a hard one, but that just meant what the skill did would be all the better. Personal experience had taught them that. And each required material they found was making their expectations soar.

"No use hanging around here. Let's head back down."

"Yes. Safely, mind you."

"We could dive off like Maple does and use my grimoire to null the damage!"

"Afraid I'm rather short on courage these days."

"Yeah…I know it would probably work, but…"

"Fair enough."

Kanade put the grimoire away, then called Sou out and showed off two other grimoires.

"We can make slides with water and ice and take those down."

"See? A safe, orthodox approach!"

"I had no idea that was possible!"

"You're like Sally!"

"I certainly match her in skill variety."

No time like the present. They moved to the pillar's edge—and a giant shadow passed overhead, as big as any dragon.

Before they could recover from the shock, a cry shook the very air.

"Whoops, the momma bird's back."

"Ha-ha, let's hurry. It seems mad."

"Kanade…!"

"Down we go!"

"Let's. This bird does not seem inclined to reason."

Kanade froze the flowing stream before the bird could attack, and they rode the spiral slide around the pillar until it reached the ground.

CHAPTER 6

Defense Build and the Charge

With the help of her guild, Maple was steadily filling in the list of required materials—and soon obtained the last of them.

Sally handed over the final items, and Maple started moving them to the designated slot in her inventory.

"I hope that's the end of it…"

"We're definitely running low on time."

For big boss battles, they could wheel out their OP twins, but prolonged gathering missions like this quest would really run out the clock.

"Well, Maple?"

"Anything different?"

"Hold on…last one…"

Maple slotted the final item, and the quest was complete—and the next one began.

"Argh, there's still more!"

"Really? Man, that's a lot."

"What is it this time?"

"Uh…it just tells me where to go!"

"That *could* be the end, then? Smells like a boss fight."

Sally had a point. When quests *just* gave a location, there was often an ambush waiting. And that usually involved a boss.

"Should we come with? Normally, you'd handle it, but in your state..."

With her skills sealed, Maple could only attack with items. If the boss was tanky or could heal itself, she'd be left high and dry.

"Whatcha thinking?"

"I'd love some company! Let me share the map."

She did just that. It showed the route they had to follow.

"Hmm? What the...?"

"Uh, curious."

"That's such a long way!"

The map showed red dots at each location they had to pass through, linked by a line. The dots were not near each other at all, and this clearly required a lot of travel time. But there were several possible routes—she could pass through all the points, or only a few of them, saving herself some time.

This was clearly a bit different from the "go here, fight a boss" quest Sally and Chrome had envisioned.

"But either way, if you can bring us along, no reason not to."

"That's true!"

The rest of her guild was clearly in for the long haul. Maple agreed that having help would be far more productive than trying to do this solo.

"If everyone's got time, I'd like to get started!"

"Yes, let's get it over with."

"Can you all help?" Maple asked.

Everyone nodded, so they set out right away.

"Haku, please."

Riding Kasumi's snake, Sally kept her map open, navigating.

"Is this the place?"

"Mm-hmm. Kasumi, stop here."

They got down. No need to scour their surroundings—the terrain in front of them stood out.

"That must be it."

"What a huge pit!"

"Can't see the bottom. Looks like you can follow the edge down..."

It was clearly very deep. Previous pit descents had been trivialized by having Maple deploy Martyr's Devotion to keep them safe as they plummeted to the bottom, but that wasn't an option here.

"Kanade, you got anything?"

"I do. Several possibilities... Which do you prefer?"

"The safest one!"

"If that's what you want, Maple, I aim to provide."

Kanade proposed a means to get them all to the bottom of the pit unharmed, and Maple nodded.

"That sounds good!"

"By your standards, Maple?"

"But it *should* be safe..."

Their nerves steeled, they gathered at the edge of the pit. This was how Maple Tree always conquered heights.

"On three!"

Maple did the countdown, and they flung themselves in. Gravity took hold, and they rocketed down, past plumes of flames and gusts of winds from things lining the walls, the floor below coming up fast.

"Guardian Ward!" Kanade cried, and light covered all of them a moment before they touched down.

There was a cracking sound, and the light vanished, the ward preventing all falling damage they would have taken.

"Feels like a waste of a good skill."

"I've got a number of damage nulls; with Maple around, I don't use them often."

Even playing solo, if he got into trouble, he rarely burned a grimoire. Kanade was fine with dying and trying again, so these spells tended to stay around in his stacks. Using this one wasn't a major loss.

"No boss here, though...?"

"Yeah. I can tell it's a good gathering point..."

Sally and Iz agreed. The walls around were lined with ores, but there seemed to be no real threats.

"Let's all look around! Maybe we'll find something!"

"Fair. Yell for Maple if you spot anything! But this could be like Glow of Deliverance on the eighth stratum, where only the player with the quest can see it—Maple, keep your eyes peeled."

"Will do!"

This place wasn't easy to get to, so they gathered what they could, scouring the bottom of the pit.

Not long after, Maple found something and called out, "Is this it?"

Maple was pointing at the wall, which had a small black swirl, slowly rotating.

"Nothing's happening?"

"Try touching it."

Just looking wasn't getting them anywhere, so Maple reached out and poked her finger in the vortex. It instantly expanded to cover the whole wall, filling the space, leaving a wavering black expanse.

"Like a portal."

"Yep."

Pushing her hand against the wall made it come alive, but she couldn't be sure what lay beyond unless she stepped in.

"Better prepare ourselves for anything before we go through."

"Right! Prep items and stuff!"

Better to waste the prep than fail to prep and lose a fight.

Once they were ready to tackle any monsters, Maple put her hand against the wall again.

Black light poured out, enveloping them. The ground beneath their feet fell away—a sign of a teleport.

"Thought so!"

"Brace yourselves!"

""Okay!""

Soon, their vision was painted black, and they found themselves in the dark. They readied their weapons, and torches on the walls began to ignite, illuminating the room.

At the back stood a giant with six arms and three faces. Each hand held a weapon. Definitely seemed like a DPS boss that hit fast and furious.

"Six arms, huh? Still..."

Sally glanced behind her. The twins each had *eight* arms. And with the items buffing them, their DPS won out.

"I'll guard them! Try to draw aggro!"

Chrome stood before the twins, while Kasumi and Sally darted off. The less of this boss's arms were aimed at Mai and Yui, the more likely they'd win.

"Wind Cutter!"

"Blood Blade!"

Each threw out a ranged attack before the boss could act, and it reacted, using its long arms to swing weapons their way.

The twins hugged the wall, and the speed fighters dodged the boss's weapons, drawing it away from their teammates.

"Multi-Cover!"

Chrome soaked blows from the rest of the arms, steadily

advancing. Only Kasumi and Sally were doing damage, so the arms were increasingly focused on them. This was what Maple Tree had been waiting for.

"Now! Run!"

""Okay!""

Chrome kept his shield up, Kanade prepped a defensive spell, and the twins ran forward.

All they had to do was get close. If this was a boss with HP—and designed to be beaten—then nothing could stand against them.

Kasumi and Sally had four arms on them. The remaining two turned toward Mai and Yui.

"That much…"

"…we can handle!"

As the weapons swung down, they raised their hammers, slamming them with perfect timing.

""Titan's Lot!""

STR surpassing all and sundry parried the boss's blows and reflected all damage back on it.

As it reeled, they stepped in closer, swinging their hammers—as six more hammers revolved around each girl.

"Ready, Mai?"

"Yep…!"

""Weapon Hurl!""

At the skill name, their weapons began to glow and spun toward the boss.

It was a skill that flung equipped weapons. Since Mai and Yui had *eight* hammers each, sixteen hammers flew at the enemy.

Ordinarily, this skill allowed ranged attacks—at a steep cost, since you no longer had your weapon. But with the twins, that didn't matter.

With a wet impact sound, one hammer after another buried itself in the boss's side. The damage was so tremendous, it reeled backward.

It didn't *matter* if they lost their weapons. This one attack alone would kill anything.

One of the last three hammers hit the boss right in the face, tearing off the head and shattering the wall behind it, and a black flame consumed its form. It crumbled and burst into light.

"They don't need to get right up to bosses anymore…"

"And if we get them a second set of hammers, they'll be rock-solid."

"With you around, Iz, they're safe even after a throw."

This might well be a great way to use up the collection of weapons slumbering in Iz's inventory.

"Wow! I didn't know you had that skill!"

"It's new! We learned it after killing lots of monsters with Farshot and Throw."

"There's no way to make it so we only throw one, though."

But having eight weapons at once was rather unique; the skill hadn't exactly been designed for their loadout. No matter how many weapons they had equipped, the downside was the same. Except…this just increased the surface area they hit, and it drastically lowered their enemy's chances of survival. It was almost always better to throw everything.

With the twins, that pretty much melted any boss without leaving them exposed.

"I doubt it was meant to be such a powerful skill…"

"But this does give us more strategic options."

One minute, Kasumi and Sally had been handling four of its arms—the next, sixteen hammers suddenly slammed into it. It had been quite a shock.

"With Mai and Yui along, it won't take that long to hit up these locations."

"If everyone's got time, think we should take the longest route? It was a long quest to begin with, so doing the completionist route might feel pretty good."

"We're up for it!"

"Yes, we can fight a while!"

"If everyone else is in!"

A series of boss fights usually took its toll, but not on Maple Tree.

With that settled, it was time for the next destination. They hopped on the magic circle to leave.

"......? Maple."

"What's up, Sally?"

"Uh…are the lines on your face getting longer?"

"Are they? I can't see them myself!"

"Might be my imagination. Could also just be something that happens as you get further along in this quest. But it could also be a time limit…? Let's keep an eye on it."

"Sure!"

With that, they followed the others out.

What followed was little more than domination. From unique landforms to proper dungeons and monsters' dens—in they stepped, and all things perished within.

Mai and Yui attacked with raw force, and without specific counters to that, nothing could stop them. No ordinary boss stood a chance.

Defeating everything in their way, they passed through the

points on the map. At last, Haku was drawing near the final point on every possible route.

"They're definitely expanding…"

The black lines had gone from Maple's face, down her back and shoulders, and had even reached her thighs. She'd double-checked her menus, but there were no status effects, no changes to her stats—so they couldn't tell if this was good or bad.

"Still no change, Maple?"

"Nope! Just visual so far!"

"Each boss we slew made it bigger…and that feels like we're making it worse."

"We've got no hints, either way, so no basis to make a judgment on."

Since they'd chosen the route with the most fights, they were either headed for the best ending…or the worst one.

Regardless, it was too late to turn back. They'd just have to finish the quest. As long as this monster couldn't negate all Mai and Yui's attacks, they'd be fine. Maple Tree wasn't really that worried.

"The map says we're almost there…"

"Right in the middle of this field? What now?"

"We'll have to get down and look."

So far, they'd always found a swirl for Maple to activate somewhere. Kasumi put Haku back in her ring, and they looked around.

This area was flat, so it was hard to imagine it would be all that well hidden. A careful search soon paid off—the mark was floating just above the ground.

"Got it, Maple! Over here!" Sally called.

Maple trotted over. As she got close, the quest was marked clear, and a new one began.

"Guess we fight a boss inside. But, uh…hng."

"Your skills?"

"Still useless."

"Another quest down, another boss… Think this is the last one?"

"We'll do our part!"

"We can beat any boss!"

Maple Tree's charge had made the twins very confident. Even if this was the strongest monster yet, it had no chance against their barrage.

"Um, but I actually have to go alone."

"Oh? We can't come with?"

"It says solo only…right, Sally?"

Sally checked the quest description and confirmed that Maple had read it right.

"Once again…your skills aren't back?"

"Nope. Only got my passives."

Since she'd been allowed to keep skills that didn't require verbal activation, her defense was alive and well—but that was all. Virtually all her offensive options were lost, and she'd been unable to contribute anything on the way there. Just plodded along behind the others. That meant she had all her Devour uses left, but it seemed unlikely that would be enough.

"So…items it is?"

"It might *not* be a boss! Be ready for anything."

The guild members put their heads together, brainstorming ideas, any means to increase her chances of victory. Iz gave her a ton of potentially useful items. Otherwise, they just had to trust Maple.

"I bet this is a very long fight. I'll tell you how it goes another day!"

If Maple had to item a boss to death, it might turn out like some of her old battles: an endurance fight, relying on her defense to survive while she chipped away at it. She didn't want to leave them all standing around that whole time.

As ready as she could be, Maple reached out—and touched the swirl.

"Hoping for good news!"

"Praying you can win!"

""Best of luck, Maple!""

"Don't worry about how many items you're using."

"Heh-heh...come back with something nifty."

"Maple! Do your worst. And win this."

Once each had said their piece, Maple nodded—and vanished into the darkness.

CHAPTER 7

Defense Build and Taboo Master

The darkness around Maple receded, and she could see once more. She found herself on a plain much like the one she'd come from.

Flat ground as far as the eye could see, no sign of forests or towns (these had been visible at the edge of the horizon before the teleport). Clearly, this would not be a battle where the terrain came into play.

As she looked around, the black marks on her body shrank away—and something took shape before her. A pale man with long white hair and a black sword on his hip.

Maple was rather relieved. He wasn't some obviously powerful grotesque creature.

"Fine work gathering the necessary sacrifices for my revival."

"Thanks!"

"Now only the final step remains: I must absorb your soul. And the mana that lies within."

"Yeah?"

He'd seemed reasonable for exactly four seconds. His about-face left Maple blinking.

Then again, the quest told her to defeat a boss. That must mean this man—there had never been a peaceful solution.

"Stand still that you might perish!"

"Argh! Hydra!"

The man drew his sword and stepped toward her as an HP bar appeared above his head.

Maple raised her shield and tried to use a skill...but no poison deluge arrived.

"Why?! You're not in me anymore!"

"Only a fool would remove your shackles."

That made sense, but Maple still puffed out her cheeks and pouted at him.

The man closed in quickly, swinging hard, moving nearly as fast as Sally. Maple tried to get her shield up, but he slipped around it, his sword slamming home. His slender build belied his surprising strength, and the force of that sword blow sent her flying.

"Whooooa!"

If she took this man at his word, his body had been crafted from the rare items they'd collected, Iz's powerful gear, and the souls of the monsters she'd slain. He would hardly be feeble. Her guild had just taken advantage of Mai and Yui's strength to clear out all the bosses they could. Naturally, this would make him even stronger.

The one upside was that he hadn't taken away Maple's defense. And his attacks didn't do piercing damage, so he couldn't get around that. This gave Maple just enough leeway to rethink her approach.

"Okay...let's do this!"

With all the support her guild had provided, she really wanted to win this for them. Maple scrambled back to her feet, eyes on the man, searching for a weakness. He seemed disinclined to lessen his offensive; closing in swiftly, he swung that mysterious black blade and sent her flying again.

"Urgh! I can't afford to waste this!"

Rolling across the ground, Maple put her great shield back in her inventory. She was heavily reliant on items right now—Devour was her best attack but also a reliable means of defense. She couldn't waste a single use.

She spent a while getting slashed across the plain but eventually got used to that, and the wheels in her brain started turning.

"I'd like to get away from him, but he's awfully fast. Hnggg…"

Each time he knocked her back, she barely managed to get to her feet before he was on her again. She couldn't exactly gain more distance by getting up and walking away.

"Do I have anything…? Oh, this might work!"

Midair, she took an item out of her inventory and rubbed it on her back. This didn't do anything obvious. The next attack was coming, but Maple didn't even get up, just lay on her back in the dirt.

Just before the sword struck home, there was a huge explosion underneath her, knocking her several feet into the air.

"Cool!"

She didn't really accomplish anything else—she just fell straight back down, slammed into the ground, and got slashed across the plain by the man once more. Yet this outcome seemed to please her immensely.

Maple had used one of Iz's handcrafted sticky bombs. While ordinary bombs would blow up the moment they took a hit, these were made of finer stuff: There was a built-in delay between sticking them to something and when they would first detonate. It wasn't possible to attach them to an enemy, which generally meant placing them around the battlefield. But it *was* possible to attach them to yourself—not something anyone else would ever want to do, and an often-forgotten feature. But for Maple in this specific moment, they were a vital way of increasing mobility.

She could attach them to herself in advance, let that delay pass, then let the bomb blow her in the other direction.

"Good! Again!"

Maple repeated the setup and lay there waiting for the explosion. Soon, there was a *boom*, and she rocketed skyward, and in midair, there was a second explosion, followed by a third, each rocketing her higher. Sticky bombs would not explode until that delay was done—one blast would not take the others out with it. By attaching them a few moments apart, she could effectively double jump and blow herself higher and higher.

A tactic only Maple could use, since neither the bombs nor the fall could hurt her. Still, it did give her the distance she wanted.

"Gotta be quick—all right!"

With Quick Change sealed, she had to manually change her gear from the inventory screen. She swapped in a piece that came with a useful passive, one that was lately proving vital to her guild's performance.

White hands appeared in the air, holding a shield. They braced it underneath Maple as she fell, catching her.

Helping Hands was a passive skill. Like Devour, one of the few skills she had left.

This let her hover in the air. She looked over the edge and found the man with his sword raised high, swinging hard.

"Whoa!"

A glittering effect came her way, matching the swing's trajectory. She hastily pulled her head back. It struck the shield beneath her and didn't touch Maple—if this attack had knockback, she couldn't afford to let it hit her.

"Before he does anything else..."

Maple pulled out more items. Once again, they were stuffed with gunpowder. And of course, this was not a means of attack but of transportation.

It was a rocket. Light the fuse, and it would blast itself sky-high. The idea was to shoot these at flying monsters, but Maple took a bunch out and secured them to her body with a rope, like a belt made of rockets.

"Liftoff!"

She cracked a fire crystal, igniting all the fuses, then stood straight up.

A moment later, she shot skyward, belching smoke.

Now she was high enough that those ranged attacks couldn't reach her. She took a seat on her shield. Perhaps the designers had assumed she couldn't get this high without skills, or wouldn't need to. Either way, the man had no way of reaching her.

"Time to fight back!"

Maple was finally ready. She took an item out of her inventory.

Specifically, a rock. Nothing special about it, just an ordinary piece of stone. She'd helped Mai and Yui gather a bunch making bases in the eighth event, and they weren't designed to fly, so the moment this left her inventory, gravity kicked in, and it plummeted downward.

"Get him!"

The man nimbly dodged the falling rock, and it sank deep into the ground, staying put. Not a direct hit, but she had far more ammunition. Not just rocks—iron balls, clumps of ice, everything big and heavy that Iz had been hauling around with her.

"There's more where that came from!"

Today's weather was boulders with a chance of steel balls and scattered ice clumps. As the ground grew buried in her detritus, Maple showed no signs of stopping.

The man was quick on his feet and tried dodging while aiming ranged attacks, but the endless rain of projectiles was slowly starting to rack up damage. Not a lot, but each hit brought him that much closer to death.

The persistence that had allowed Maple to eat a dragon was alive and well. For over an hour, she calmly dropped things on the man, knocking a solid 20 percent off his HP.

"Whew...I think I'm hitting more often!"

The ground below was no longer flat—the footing was highly uneven, and his movement options were limited. The increasing hit rate proved this, and given another four hours, she'd likely manage to defeat him.

But that hope didn't last. Black light wreathed his body, then burst, and devilish wings emerged from his back.

These flapped once, and he took off, wheeling about until he was flying directly at Maple.

"Yikes?!"

She'd made clever use of her items to get herself there but had no means of matching a flying foe.

"No, don't...augh!"

He was swiftly above her, and his downward slash sent Maple plummeting headfirst to the ground below.

She hit the ground with a crash that sent plumes of dust into the air, but she knew full well fall damage never hurt her. She was soon on her feet, running.

"Gotta prep the next thing!"

If this boss could fly now, her "drop things on him" strategy was kaput. She needed a new plan to get through the remaining 80 percent.

With no skills, one good way to hurt a fast foe was to secure

a position where she could attack without interruption until she scored a hit.

Her other approach was waiting for the foe to come to her, which worked great against monsters.

Naturally, the man didn't land as hard as she did, but his descent was by no means slow. She didn't have much time until he caught up.

If she got stuck in the knockback loop again, she'd have a hard time getting out—she had to make the most of this moment.

"Okay...yes!"

Putting her back to one of the boulders she'd dropped, she took a few more out of her inventory, placing them around her. Then she put one more on top so the only gap was in front of her. Then she waited. No player would ever step in there, but monsters would.

And that difference gave her a huge advantage.

Soon, the man came in, the darkness in her niche making the glow on his sword evident. She might not be good at dodging, but when she knew when and where an opponent was coming and was ready for it, Maple had enough experience to match that timing.

Like Sally always did, she half-turned, letting the thrust pass by her, and as it retreated, she swung both hands.

In the darkness, her pitch-black shield glimmered. It swallowed the shoulder, neck, and head, doing major damage. Black light gathered, swiftly restoring the man's form—but not healing the damage done.

"Gah...!"

The man reeled back, and Maple tried thrusting her shield out to strike again, but the man had gone out of reach and was quickly backpedaling to recover. Outside Maple's niche, she couldn't hit him.

"Well, I'll be waiting right here!"

Maple saw no point in pursuing. She could simply wait in the trap she'd made, countering when he came to her.

The man *had* to defeat her. He was made that way. Only Maple had the option of quitting the battle—he was forced to come to her. Into the monster's lair.

In he came. The monster's maw awaited. Her jaws struck even more accurately. This time, she bit him twice.

But the monster—Maple—did not look pleased.

"Seven more..."

The man leaped back out of the hole. His HP had diminished, but at this rate, even if she landed every Devour, that alone wouldn't be enough to finish this.

That wasn't too surprising. Devour was a high-damage skill, but this was a boss who'd been hit by a hundred boulders and only lost 20 percent of his health.

"Maybe I'd better save the rest!"

Odds were he would add more attacks as his health diminished. If she needed to rush to a finish, she'd need Devour. She put her shield away and took out some oil and a crystal to ignite it.

Flames went up all around her, turning her vicinity into a damage zone. She squinted through it, waiting for the man to lunge at her again—but this time, he didn't.

"Huh?"

Unlike Devour, the flames were already generating damage. The boss's AI was set to avoid areas that would obviously hurt him.

"So fire won't work..."

If she had to deal damage at the last second, that meant bombs or the elemental items she often made use of.

She put a crystal in each hand and waited for the fire to go out.

The moment it did, the man lunged at her. With the entrance

accidentally narrowed, she'd effectively baited this lunge and was able to dodge it with ease.

As she dodged, she leaned forward, hands thrust out. The crystals cracked, and fire and lightning leaped from her hands. These did damage, but much less than Devour. The man was soon back on the offensive.

"Ack! R-right..."

The delay between blows had been a side effect of Devour—with her shield stowed, she took the hit and was slammed into the back wall.

"Wh-whoa! Hey!"

He was really whaling away at her, and the air filled with clanging noises, but none of it hurt. Still, the powerful knockback was just as strong as before, so she couldn't exactly move. Helping Hands was still holding that shield, but the boss was right on top of her, and she couldn't wedge it between them. Before she could think of anything, the boulder behind her proved less durable than Maple herself. There was a loud *crack*, and it crumbled—and Maple was sent flying away. She'd used one of the outer boulders on the heap she'd dropped, so even if one crumbled, she was still in a little cul-de-sac.

The rock she'd used as a roof lost its support and fell, leaving the man and Maple completely surrounded by boulders.

"......!"

That would have doomed anyone else, but to Maple, it was a stroke of luck.

"Hmm...hyah!"

The flurry of blows kept her pinned to the rock behind, but she was just able to get into her inventory and take out an iron ball to place above them. With rocks blocking them in all directions and a giant steel ball overhead, there was no escape.

The ball fell, pressing down on both Maple and the man. She

was trying to crush him to death. With the ball's weight on him, the man *was* taking steady damage. But so little it was hard to be sure it was actually happening. Still, after several hours of this, it would certainly add up.

Naturally, the man wasn't about to stand there and let himself be crushed. He was trying to escape.

Unable to move, he started using magic, firing spells from his pinned blade at the ball above.

But each time it shattered, Maple took out another, keeping them both crushed.

Since only the boss was taking damage from this, as long as she kept it up, victory would be hers. A very long, winding road to victory, but it would get her there.

An hour and change into her "crush the boss to death" strategy, a new issue cropped up.

She was running out of items to crush him with.

Iz had given her everything she could, but they hadn't been intended for this scenario, and she did not have the quantity it required. No other players had ever found themselves at an impasse due to lack of fatal crushing boulders.

It would be nice if she could collect the boulders she'd dropped before, but Maple herself was trapped in the vice, so that wasn't an option.

A second hour passed, and she was steadily running low on items.

She'd managed to shave off another 20 percent, but was still quite far from victory. In time, the boulders she dropped would vanish.

Trying to get his health down as far as she could while she had him trapped, she kept going.

It would have been nice if she could use bombs, but those would break the walls around her—the slow but steady route was her only option.

At last, she ran out of applicable items. While the man busied himself attacking the boulder above, she figured since this was the last one, she might as well start start throwing out all her bombs. She had nothing else to crush him with, so there was little use keeping him pinned with her. And this was likely her last chance to blow him up.

Once every last crevice was stuffed with bombs, one of the man's blows triggered one, and they all went up together.

Boulders and balls weren't really intended as offensive tools, so the bombs did way more damage. All of them scored a clean hit, and the boss lost another 10 percent of his health. But the walls around them could hardly stand up to that destruction; they were blown away. And the first batch she'd dropped had timed out and vanished. When the blast ended, she found herself back on the flat plain with the boss.

Half the boss's health was left. This was clearly another phase shift: Black energy emanated from the dust cloud.

Figuring this meant new attacks, she equipped another shield—one of Iz's unclaimed stash—then handed Helping Hands two more. Firming up her defenses.

When the man shot out of the dust, he now had a sword in each hand. These were wreathed in billowing black energy, like flames. Sensing danger, Maple tensed up.

More damage and side effects—if the visuals changed, that meant something.

Maple braced for a charge, but the man swung his arms, generating a magic circle. This changed everything.

A black laser shot at Maple, and she blocked it with a shield, which turned black. Maple's eyes widened, and the black shield exploded, leaving a gap in her phalanx. The shield was held by Helping Hands, so she'd avoided a fumble, but if she'd been holding the shield, she'd likely have dropped it.

The boss didn't leave this opening unpunished. He closed in, thrusting into the space where the shield had been.

"Urgh!"

Each place a blow landed marked her gear with black energy that soon detonated, crushing her equipment. And not just that—it was doing damage that ignored her defense, steadily carving away at her HP. Since the shields Iz gave her provided a bonus to HP, and she'd prioritized those, the three of them kept her a long way from death—but if this kept up for much longer, she was in trouble.

Maple adjusted her shields' positions, took some sticky bombs from the inventory, and stuck them to her chest.

Blocking the furious combo, she got herself righted, and the blast sent her rocketing backward.

It was no longer safe to let him slash away at her up close. Maple left her inventory open, slapping new bombs on her chest each time they exploded.

She couldn't fine-tune her movements, but each one moved her away from the boss.

And Maple was all about explosive attacks. Her open inventory let her smoothly pull out more bombs, and she scattered more in her wake each time she was blown backward.

These blasts were hurting the man as he gave chase. She had plenty of bombs left. Now she just had to avoid messing up the blast distance. One blunder would stick her in a combo, and if she couldn't right herself in time for the next bomb, death would come knocking.

"Okay! Focus!"

She took a deep breath, like Sally did. She'd come this far, and she didn't want to lose now. She braced all three shields.

She may have found a solution, but it was a spur-of-the-moment plan, not something she'd ever practiced doing. Working her inventory and throwing bombs at her enemy weren't exactly polished actions. Since the rest of her skills were sealed off, she didn't have much else to think about, but Maple was hanging on by the skin of her teeth.

Her fingers fumbled the inventory, she didn't get a bomb on her chest in time, and the man caught up.

"Yikes! No…urgh!"

In close, the boss had the advantage. Swift blows tore her up, and damage sparks flew.

"Get off me!"

At last, the bomb detonated, and she was away from him. She made a wall with her shields, not letting him take the shortest route, buying more time.

"Stick a bomb on me…drink a potion…"

One item after another, getting herself back in action. Fortunately, the ground was flat, so she could just rocket backward forever without any need for fine-tuning her path. She was keeping this combat approach under her control by eliminating any distractions.

The boss fired that explosion-generating black laser, and Helping Hands blocked it a safe distance from Maple herself. Carefully handling his attacks, doing damage in return—but each time her concentration wavered, he caught up and hit her.

Still, he was being far less effective than her.

As long as Maple still had potions, she could recover, while he could not.

"Once more!"

As he lunged at her, she scattered a bunch of bombs. Not really thinking about type or side effects, just going for volume high enough that he couldn't dodge. The moment he stepped into the area, she sparked flames, and they all went up. The blast hit her, too, but hurt only the boss—and sent her flying back.

"Whew…haah… Okay!"

The boss's HP was at 40 percent, and the fight had been going for three hours.

She'd been in several prolonged fights, but never this frenzied— she was starting to get very tired.

But she kept herself focused, and the bombs kept doing damage. Her chief concern was the number of sticky bombs: She was blowing through them fast to keep herself moving, and she had nothing that could replace them.

A little over thirty percent left. She didn't have enough sticky bombs to get through that. But if she slowed at all, he would start cutting her up, and she would likely die.

"I've gotta get Devour on him…"

She had seven uses left. If she could land them all, this would be over.

Maple decided to make that her ploy once she was sure he was below 30 percent.

She figured that would be the last phase shift—if he had anything past that, odds were the Devour combo would prevent her from ever seeing it. If he didn't have enough HP left to survive Devour, she didn't need to worry about later phases.

Red flames from her bombs and the man's black laser lit the battlefield as they each did damage.

"How's this?!"

There was an extra-large explosion. Fires billowed around the man, reducing his HP still further, and it hit that 30 percent mark.

And it *did* change his attack pattern. She hadn't wanted that but had seen it coming.

He leaped several yards in the air and deployed a giant magic circle around himself. The instant she saw that, Maple got herself as far away as she could. It was definitely not going to go her way.

She topped up her HP and swapped out the Helping Hands shields for ones with maxed-out durability. As she finished that, pitch-black goop began spewing out of the magic circle.

"It is time…for you to die!"

With that pronouncement, the man aimed his sword at Maple, and grotesque creatures began to emerge from the goop. They looked a lot like Maple's Atrocity form. Some had wings and bulging muscles, others had extra arms or legs—but all of them were wreathed in that black energy that had been damaging Maple.

"……!"

Maple took one look at them and switched to Night's Facsimile. She was in no state to handle this horde and draw things out. She'd played every trick in the book to get this far, but that approach had its limits; sheer quantity and quality would soon overwhelm her strategy. In which case, she need only bring the curtains down with her strongest—and only—weapon.

Fortunately, she was a solid distance out. She had time before the monsters reached her.

Maple quickly prepped a rocket belt and lit the fuse.

There was a *boom*, and she shot skyward. With monsters everywhere, she'd never reach the man on the ground, so she had to get him to come to her. Just as she had been.

Up here, only the winged monsters—and the man himself—could follow her.

The man could fly far faster than any of the monsters he'd summoned, but they'd been closer, so they got to her first.

"......!"

These flying monsters were in her way, preventing her from slamming her great shield into the boss. But if she dropped back down, she'd be gobbled up. With no time to hang around thinking and no other options, she just had to stick to this plan.

The rocket-powered ascent petered out, and she started to fall.

She adjusted her posture, falling directly toward the monsters and vaporizing one of them with Devour. That opened a path, and she fell through the flock at full speed.

Beyond them was the boss—her real target.

His blade swung, and Maple thrust out her shield. Swords or sorcery, no matter how destructive they were, they were powerless before her shield.

The first hit swallowed up his weapon. With nothing left standing between them, her all-consuming shield scored a direct hit on his body.

Maple was thoroughly versed in Devour technique. She knew she'd go right through the man, so she had Helping Hands put two shields just under him for her to stand on and managed to land on that with a loud *clang*.

The man could rebuild his body after Devour swallowed it up, but that did not negate the damage done. This took him a moment, which was her opportunity.

"Hyah!"

She'd landed right behind him, and she began waving her shield back and forth like a pendulum, repeatedly slamming it into him. Busy reforming, he could not get away.

Maple slammed every Devour use she had into the man—and

realized he still had a sliver of health. She'd been forced to use one Devour elsewhere, and that had made her come up short.

Still, he had *very* little HP left. Bombs and items should get her through that.

But while she was taking those out, the monsters she'd dropped past caught up and attacked, preventing her from throwing anything out.

And their attacks came with a small measure of fixed damage, ignoring her defense and chipping away at her health.

"Get…off me!"

Unable to throw the bombs, she wrapped her arms around them and curled herself up, soaking the full force of the explosion and knocking herself out of the horde toward the ground. The extra HP her shields provided had let her cling to life. She quickly grabbed a crystal from her inventory and used it, putting her health back out of danger.

The man had finished repairing his body. As she fell, Maple saw him spread his wings, diving after her—coming to finish this.

He had the positional advantage. If she hit the ground, the monsters waiting for her would never let her go.

This was literally her last chance.

The man was coming headlong at her. She focused on his sword, a small bomb in her hand. One of Iz's handmade specialties: a limited blast radius but very high damage. Enough to kill him—if she could land the hit.

But no matter how focused she was, Maple could not dodge this strike. She didn't have Sally's knack for evasion, and this situation did not allow for flukes.

If she couldn't dodge her way to an opening, then—

As the sword neared, she placed a floating shield behind her, at a slight angle. Her back hit it, stopping her fall, and she gritted her teeth.

A moment later, the sword cut deep. Damage sparks flew, and the knockback slammed her against the shield.

Not the most stable of walls—there was a *clang*, her body bounced, and her face twisted in pain.

But she kept her eyes facing front. As the swing completed, she used that small bounce to kick off her shield, launching herself up. A tiny gap before the next attack—time enough for her to thrust out her hand.

Maple couldn't do what Sally could, but she could do what Sally couldn't.

Her defense had saved her time and time again, ensuring she need not worry about collateral damage from her own attacks.

As the man charged, she used the rebound from the knockback to place herself right up against him.

Too close for him to get away, in range of a blast no other player could risk standing near.

"Eh-heh-heh, how ya like that?"

Maple grinned triumphantly—and the blast enveloped them both. In the ensuing sound and fury, only one of them perished.

Not long after, outside the game, where the developers were hard at work—

They had it set up so an alert would go off if specific hidden dungeons or questlines were cleared, and once again, that distinctive *ding* echoed through the room.

"Who did what?"

"The forbidden tome…"

The man checking the logs made a face.

"Who?"

"Maple."

"…………???"

Everyone in earshot looked baffled. That should not have been possible—not with the boss they'd made and the quests leading to it.

"I must be hearing things. Say that again."

"……It was Maple."

"……But how?"

"Gonna have to see this for myself…"

"How would the seal work on her?"

"She won't count as a mage, so it's Pattern A."

"Then she'll only have passives! That would let her keep her defense, but how would she actually *win*?!"

"Let's watch the start of the fight."

Everyone turned to the screen, watching intently. Odds were high she'd found some weird exploit to win.

The fight started normally enough, with the boss aggressively attacking. Not doing damage but not letting her get up.

"Figured she could tank that."

"That's her thing."

After a while, Maple started using bombs. This let her gain some distance and use Helping Hands to hover above the fight—which made everyone groan.

"Aha…"

"I've scanned ahead, and she spends the next hour dropping rocks…"

"Good lord. Why did she even have that many?"

"Who knows…?"

Not long after, the boss started flying. The developers knew this would hardly be the end of it.

As the video played on, a stir ran round the room.

"It's theoretically possible… Sticky bombs, huh?"

"I didn't see Maple pulling off something that technical. Was that her thing?"

"Maybe Sally taught it to her. It seems like something she'd do…"

"Without Iz's backup…"

"Clearly, the whole guild pitched in on this one. That's how she cleared the gathering quests so quick."

Maple was no longer on her own. With help, she could make the impossible possible. A far cry from the days when she'd been forced to spend hours eating a dragon.

"Wow, she's really got moves."

"Not taking damage is key. If anyone else tried that, it'd be suicide."

This was no unexpected bug or a victory claimed through abusing an exploit. This was a fair fight, achieved through a clear understanding of her own strengths, using a ton of resources and time.

"All about them passives."

"Yup."

"Is that the issue here? This skill…"

"……………"

The root of her evil. Behind all Maple's actions lay that exceptional defense—and this incident forced them to acknowledge that again.

With her very long fight over, it was time for the final preparations. Maple was visiting the Order of the Holy Sword's Guild Home, in her capacity as Maple Tree's guild master. Talking to their guild master—Pain.

"Then we are allies. Do you have a preference on which side we take?"

"Um, I don't really, no. Do you?"

"The monster placements remain unchanged. Thus, it is better to side against the monsters you can easily handle."

"Aha...then I bet Velvet goes with the fire side."

"Velvet? From Thunder Storm?"

"She's said she's siding against me."

"I see. In that case..."

As they discussed things, in another room, Frederica, Drag, and Dread were awaiting the outcome on a nearby couch.

"A team-up with Maple's crew..."

"Yo, that ain't settled yet."

"Ain't like it's a bad offer for them."

"I know, right?"

Not long after, the door swung open, and the two leaders emerged.

"Pain, what's the word?"

"Our alliance is settled. In accordance with that, we've decided which camp to take."

Inform all guild members, insist this information be kept secret—and with those orders, they dispersed.

"Well, that's a plus to our efforts."

"Yeah, looking forward to it. And...those black marks are gone."

"I noticed! I bet something went down."

"Too many witnesses—we weren't just seeing things."

"Yeah, I'm guessing she finished some sort of secret quest. It likely made her far stronger."

"Good news! Anything that makes it easier for us."

"Hello? We need to prove that everyone else can rely on the Order."

"Ha-ha-ha! This'll be a blast!"

No one had seen Maple use anything game-changing since Machine God and Atrocity. But everyone figured she had secrets.

If she was on their side, they could pin their hopes on those.

"Time for the final prep. Once the event begins, it'll be chaos."

"Yup, yup."

"Roger that."

"We'll do what we can."

This was a PvP event. The Order had no intention of losing. They were ready to do whatever it took to emerge victorious.

As the alliance between Maple Tree and the Order firmed up, other guilds were finalizing their plans.

Flame Empire, too, was putting the intel they'd gathered to use, firming up their strategies, and picking a side.

"So, Mii, I found something cool here…"

"Interesting. That means…"

"Oh, I didn't think of that! Anything else?"

"Hmm. I discovered several others…and I bet not many other people did. Maybe just me."

Marx pointed out several locations.

"Always possible they've been found and everyone's keeping them secret…but it doesn't hurt to bear them in mind."

"Your skill helped you find them, right, Marx? I've never seen anyone else who can do what you do, so this is probably a big deal."

"Yeah...?"

"Indeed. Let us share it with the guild. Which will affect the side we take..."

"Yeah. Namely..."

"Hmm, I'd prefer that side myself."

"Agreed. It will bring out our strength."

"Sounds like we're on the same page. Based on this intel, I'll inform them of our choice of camps. All members are free to make their own decisions in light of that."

"But I bet we know what they'll say."

"Yep."

"Mm-hmm."

"O-oh?"

These three would definitely side with Mii—and so would most of their guild. If the choice didn't matter, why not follow their leader?

"In that case, let's aim for the victory!"

"All right...!"

"Yeah!"

"Absolutely!"

Their strength in group events was real. Flame Empire had their plans drawn. They'd made no advance allies—but the Order was not the only guild who did.

Specifically—Thunder Storm and Rapid Fire.

"It certainly is big."

"Rapid Fire's a major guild...but I don't believe the scale is that different from ours."

"Over here. Come on in."

Lily led Velvet and Hinata into a meeting room, and they took seats around the table.

Wilbert was waiting for them. Only the four leaders were present.

"Let's talk."

"Ha-ha, you're on your best behavior? Almost strange to see that now. But given the venue, I suppose it's appropriate."

With that, Lily got the conversation on track.

"It seems some guilds have already locked their plans. Naturally, we can't count on that, but we don't believe there's much discrepancy in the standings."

In other words, whichever camp could field the most players with game-changer skills would have the advantage.

"What do you say? Have you changed your mind?"

"Velvet?"

"But of course. We fight together."

"That is what we want to hear. With Thunder Storm on our side, victory draws that much closer."

"Excellent. That's why we came here today."

"Good to know. Then we'll spare you the lengthy pitch."

"But we do have one condition."

"……Name it."

Velvet wasn't the strategic type, so the word *condition* made Lily tense up.

Like she could hardly stand the anticipation, Velvet grinned—and put her hands on the table, leaning in.

"We wanna fight Maple!"

"……Ha-ha, I should have known. Naturally, we've done our homework accordingly and are in complete agreement."

"Then we good!"

"Your true colors are showing. So this is the real *you*."

"That's all she cares about…so we've got no other major concerns."

"Then let's move on to the specifics. We'll need to be prepared for the stronger players, or our lines will crumble fast."

"Yes… I'm in charge of defense. Ask away…as long as I can ask, too."

Their focus on individual players showed their confidence against numbers. If they prepared for someone capable of overturning those odds, they could maintain an advantage in this event, where the total number of survivors could change the outcome.

"Like, what should I do?"

"Rush the enemy. That's where your strengths lie."

"I know, but…ain't we got any schemes?"

"We'll consider them."

Where and when to send her was critical. Velvet, Hinata, and Wilbert could all turn a battle around. Lily turned her thoughts to predicting the event flow and how to change it.

◆□◆□◆□◆□◆

As all players made their final adjustments, counting down to the event, the big day finally arrived. Maple Tree gathered early, making their final checks.

"Gotta keep an eye on this area…and here. Nasty monsters here…"

Sally was leading the briefing. The admins had not announced which guilds were on which side, and their information was incomplete, but any players not seen in town today were likely against them.

"I'm sure Thunder Storm kept their word and are against us. Mai, Yui, Kanade, watch out."

These three were low-level and had little in the way of defense—a poor match against Velvet's wild lightning storms.

After running down the players they had marked, the final countdown began.

"Okay, everyone! Let's do our best!"

"Yeah! I'll go anywhere that needs defending."

""We'll do what we can!""

"We know it. Just be careful."

"I'm going to use a lot of grimoires this time."

"I'll keep you all supplied. Fall back if you're in trouble."

"Anything you wanna know, ask, and I'll tell you."

They all said their piece, and the light of the transport spell appeared around them. The event map was the same map—but a different instance of it.

"Okay! Let's win this, Sally!"

"......That's the plan."

Sally focused, and Maple put her game face on.

They were whisked off to the event map—a grand-scale PvP war, where all their skills and strength would be put to the test.

AFTERWORD

Hello to anyone who stumbled across Volume 13 and picked it up. A heartfelt thank-you to anyone who's been following the series from the start. I am Yuumikan.

Here we are, in Volume 13. The story has taken us to the ninth stratum—and that serves as a reminder of just how much I've written.

Counting from the start of the web version, I've been at this for six years now. A long time by any standard.

When I started writing, I had no idea so many changes would take place. Naturally, I wrote words and put them where people could see them, so I certainly hoped people would find it, but I never imagined there would be this many.

But as a result, I've experienced so many things I never saw coming. The manga uses all manner of facial expressions to show how much the characters enjoy the game. It could not be a better adaptation. The anime did a fantastic job of translating the action to the screen and pleased everyone who'd read the novels.

I've said this before, but I have been blessed with who I've worked with. And naturally, that includes my readers. I may be feeling wistful now, but Maple's adventure will continue unabated, so I hope you continue to enjoy it.

The more time passes, the more you want to look back.

I believe there will be more information about the anime's second season in due time, so look forward to that. The broadcast is in the not-too-distant future, and I intend to enjoy it with all of you.

I have so much to say that I could write forever, but I'll wrap things up here.

The anime seemed so far off, but now it's almost here.

I want to revel in their adventures, so let's all enjoy them together.

And I hope you're looking forward to Volume 14!

Yuumikan